GUS

SATAN'S FURY MC- MEMPHIS

L. WILDER

Gus
Satan's Fury MC- Memphis
Copyright 2019 L. Wilder
All rights reserved.

BookBub- https://www.bookbub.com/authors/l-wilder

L. Wilder's Newsletter (sign up for giveaways and news about upcoming releases) http://eepurl.com/dvSpW5

Editor: Lisa Cullinan

Proofreader- Rose Holub www.facebook.com/ReadbyRose/

Proofreader- Honey Palomino

Personal Assistant: Natalie Weston PA

Catch up with the entire Satan's Fury MC Series today!

All books are FREE with Kindle Unlimited!

Summer Storm (Satan's Fury MC Novella)

Maverick (Satan's Fury MC #1)

Stitch (Satan's Fury MC #2)

Cotton (Satan's Fury MC #3)

Clutch (Satan's Fury MC #4)

Smokey (Satan's Fury MC #5)

Big (Satan's Fury #6)

Two Bit (Satan's Fury #7)

Diesel (Satan's Fury #8)

Blaze (Satan's Fury Memphis Chapter)

Shadow (Satan's Fury Memphis Chapter)

Riggs (Satan's Fury Memphis Chapter)

Murphy (Satan's Fury Memphis Chapter)

Damaged Goods- (The Redemption Series Book 1- Nitro)

Max's Redemption (The Redemption Series Book 2- Max)

Inferno (Devil Chasers #1)

Smolder (Devil Chaser #2)

Ignite (Devil Chasers #3)

Consumed (Devil Chasers #4)

Combust (Devil Chasers #5)

❀ Created with Vellum

GUS

*C*lub life isn't for everyone, but for me—it was everything. I started prospecting for Satan's Fury MC when I was twenty-one years old, and right from the start, I knew there was no other place for me. I dedicated my life to the brothers of the Washington Chapter—my family. Through the years, they taught me everything I needed to know—not just about MC life, but about the kind of man I wanted to be. I wanted to be a man who demonstrated loyalty, pride, and grit. I wanted my brothers, and those around me, to know that I was someone they could trust, that I would always hold true to my word, and that I'd never waiver or show signs of weakness when it came to my commitment to the club and its prosperity. I'd felt honored that my brothers had seen those very qualities in me when they voted me in as their sergeant-at-arms. I thought I would end out my days there with them in Washington, but Saul, the club's president, had other plans for me.

We'd just been dismissed from church when Sauk

asked me to join him in the bar for a beer. I followed him over to the counter, and after I grabbed us each a cold one and sat down next to him. He took a quick pull, then said, "Butch called last night. He was just checking in, and we got to talking. We both think it's about time for us to start gaining some territory down south."

Butch was the president of the original Satan's Fury chapter in Utah. At the time, their chapter was twice the size of ours, and it was steadily growing, with at least six prospects ready to patch in. Butch and Saul created Fury in their vision, and I was curious to hear what they had planned. "Sounds like a good idea. What do you have in mind?"

"Right now, we have chapters in Washington, Utah, Colorado, Oklahoma and as of recently, Kansas, so it makes sense to keep moving further south." He pulled out his pack of smokes, and as he lit a cigarette and continued, "I'm thinking it'll probably be Memphis, but there's always Little Rock or Birmingham."

"Memphis is thriving, and it's sitting right on the Mississippi River."

"That's what I was thinking. We looked into some local chapters there but aren't sure they're worthy of the Fury name. Butch and I both agreed that it would be smarter to send some of our own down to get things started. Check out surrounding clubs and see if any might be worth patching over. We just need someone we can trust to make it happen."

"Okay, so what does any of this have to do with me?"

"Everything." He took a drag off his cigarette and smoke billowed around him as he continued, "We think you're that person, Gus. You've proven your loyalty to the club. You've got a good head on your shoulders, and you're a born leader. We both think you have what it takes to get things rolling down there. That is … if you're up for it."

"I'm up for whatever you need me to do. You know that." While I was flattered that Saul asked me to take on such a vital task, I didn't let it go to my head. I knew a lot was taken into consideration when they chose me, like the fact that I was not only experienced, but I was single with no strong ties to outside family. Regardless, I was grateful that I'd been chosen to lead the new chapter, and I'd do everything in my power to make it a success. "I'm just going to need a little direction here. What exactly is it that you're wanting me to do?"

"We'd want you to go there as the president of the new chapter and get things started. Find a location for the clubhouse, check out other clubs, and look for potential patch overs. Draw in some new prospects. Establish some work fronts. The whole nine yards." When Saul saw the look of concern on my face, he smiled and said, "Don't worry. We won't be shipping you out there alone. Butch will be sending one his best to be there at your side, along with a few members and prospects from both chapters."

I couldn't hide my enthusiasm when I answered, "I'd be honored, Prez."

"I was hoping you'd say that."

"You have any idea on when you want this to go down?"

"The sooner the better." He put out his cigarette and continued, "I'll get back with Butch later tonight and let him know you're on board. We'll talk it over, and once we have more of the details sorted, we'll discuss it with the others during church."

"Thank you for this opportunity, Prez. I won't let you down."

"I know you won't. That's why you were chosen." Saul finished off his beer, then stood to leave. "Best get your things in order."

Giving me a pat on the shoulder, he walked out of the bar, leaving me alone with my thoughts. It was hard not to feel pumped about the opportunity I'd been given, but as I sat there thinking about all the things that would need to be done, I started to question whether or not I was prepared to take on such an overwhelming endeavor. By the following morning, Saul confirmed that Memphis would be the location for the new chapter. At the end of the week, the brothers threw us a kick-ass farewell celebration, wanting to wish us well and congratulate me on my new position as President of the Memphis chapter. Once I'd recovered from the festivities, I packed up the rest of my belongings and headed south.

My mind was racing as I drove down the interstate. While I was eager to move to Memphis and get things started, I was feeling a little apprehensive. There was a lot weighing on the success of this new chapter, and I didn't want to let Saul or my brothers down.

Luckily, I wouldn't have to take on such a huge responsibility alone. Moose, along with his old lady, Louise, their two-year-old daughter, Rayne, and Cyrus from the Utah chapter, as well as Bane, Widow, Half-Pint, and T-Bone from ours, were following close behind me as I continued towards Memphis. Once we got to Tennessee, they would be right there at my side to help get things rolling.

As soon as we hit the city limits, we found a place to stay and set to work. I'd like to say that everything went exactly as planned, that we didn't have a single hiccup, but I'd be lying. We ran into one obstacle after the next, but thankfully, it wasn't anything that couldn't be handled. We kept pushing forward, and after a few weeks' time, we'd started to make some real progress. We'd purchased an old train depot that was located on the east end of downtown right on the banks of the Mississippi River. The place needed some work, but it was the perfect size and the location couldn't have been better for our clubhouse. After spending the entire day busting our asses on some of the renovations, we all met up at one of the local pizza places to grab dinner.

The waitress had just brought over our drinks when Moose turned to me and asked, "You got any thoughts on what you want to do about the exterior fence?"

"It's gotta be at least a ten-feet with electric gates at the front and the back."

Moose was in his early thirties, and big as a fucking ox with bulging biceps and tattoos from head to toe. He was the Utah chapter's enforcer, and I'd learned early on that he wasn't a man who was afraid to speak his mind. I wasn't at all surprised when he argued, "You sure we're gonna need all that? Back in Utah, we only have a six-and-a-half-foot fence, and with the additional barbed-wire, it's been more than enough."

"Yeah, and it's located on the outskirts of Davis County in a fairly safe neighborhood. That's not the case here. Memphis has gangs at every corner." My voice grew more forceful as I told him, "As soon as they realize that we're encroaching on their territory, they're gonna be out for fucking blood, so if that means we have to put in a ten-foot security fence with barbed-wire, install a high-tech security system, and have guards posted around the clock, then that's what we're gonna fucking do."

With an almost defeated expression, he nodded and answered, "Understood."

"We're getting close." Trying to ease the tension, I told him, "It won't be long before we're out of that fucking hotel and into the clubhouse."

"Can't happen soon enough," he grumbled. "I can barely breathe in that tiny box of a room and having Louise and Rayne in such close quarters isn't helping."

"At least she doesn't fucking snore like T-Bone," Cyrus complained from across the table. He was Louise's brother, and while he was barely twenty-one and the youngest of the mix, he wasn't the least bit intimidated by anyone sitting at that table. Cyrus spoke his mind and didn't give a damn who he pissed off. "It's like I'm sleeping next to a fucking bear."

"Who said she doesn't snore?" Moose chuckled. "Hell, your sister's been sawing timbers since the first night."

"Yeah, well, the snoring's one thing, but the gas he's been letting blow all week is another. It's like something died in his fucking gut." Cyrus yawned before he added, "I haven't slept worth a damn since we got here."

"It's not that bad," T-Bone, the jokester of the group, actually sounded a little bothered by Cyrus's comment. He'd only been prospecting for a couple of months, but in the short time he'd been with us, T-Bone had proven himself worthy as a brother, never failing to make himself available when we needed him. His eyes narrowed as he continued, "And just so you know, you're not exactly easy to live with either, brother. Your clothes and shit are all over the floor, and there's never any clean towels. I don't get it. What the hell are you doing with them? Do you take three fucking showers a day or what?"

Before Cyrus could respond, our waitress came over and placed our pizzas down on the table. As everyone started to fill their plates with food, Cyrus turned to me and asked, "So, what's going on with the diner?"

We'd bought a small place right on the corner of Beale Street, but we hadn't started working on any renovations. "Nothing right now. We need to make a final decision on what we're going to do."

"Louise says simple is always better." Moose added, "I'm telling ya, brother, she knows her shit. Give her a few months, and with Cyrus's help, she can make a real go of it. Daisy Mae's will be the talk of the city."

I looked at the others and asked, "You guys good with Daisy Mae's Cafe?"

"An all-American-style café with checkered tablecloths and pictures of all the great legends of Memphis plastered on the walls: Elvis, B.B. King, Aretha Franklin, Morgan Freeman, Cybil Shepherd, and Isaac Hayes. Hell, yeah. No one would ever suspect that it's a front," Bane agreed.

When the others nodded in agreement, I said, "Then, it's settled. Daisy Mae's it is. Tell Louise to get the ball rolling."

"Consider it done."

"Before she gets started, we'll need to make sure the electrical and plumbing is up to code," Half-pint warned. Over the past few weeks, his experience with all the ins and outs of construction had been invaluable. For a prospect, he'd saved us a lot of headaches. "And once we get a construction plan together, we'll need to get the necessary permits."

"Agreed. I already checked all the zoning codes, so we should be able to get the permits without any issue. It'll pass inspection, but we all know that doesn't mean a damn thing." I leaned back in my chair and crossed my arms. "I'll go by there tonight and check things out. If all looks good, we'll get the city inspector to come down to see if he'll give us the go-ahead."

"While you're doing that, we'll head back over to the clubhouse and finish up some painting," Moose offered.

"It's been a long day, brother. You boys go back to the hotel and get some rest." As I stood up, I placed enough money on the table to cover the bill and the tip, then told them, "We'll get things finished up in the morning."

"You got it."

After I said my goodbyes, I walked out of the restaurant and headed towards my bike in the parking lot. Every muscle in my body ached as I swung my leg over the seat and started the engine. I was so tempted to put off checking the pipes until morning, but knowing I'd just end up regretting it, I pushed myself forward. Thankfully, as soon as I pulled out onto the main road, the cool night air started working its magic on me, and it wasn't long before the tension I'd been carrying with me all day started to fade. I'd always liked riding in the city, seeing all the bright lights and the people wandering along the streets, but there was something about Memphis that took that feeling to a whole new level. Cruising around the birthplace of Rock & Roll, seeing the Arkansas bridge with all its lights, and hearing the Blues down on Beale Street that just got to me like no other city ever had. By the time I made it to the diner, my spirits had lifted, and I was feeling optimistic about our club's future.

I checked inside and was pleased to see that I was right about the plumbing and electric. They both seemed to be in good condition, and I didn't see any reason why we wouldn't pass inspection. Relieved, I locked everything up and headed back out to my bike. I was just about to start the engine when my attention was drawn to a man and woman who were arguing across the street. Something didn't seem right, so I got off my bike and started towards them.

As I got closer, I was able to see them both better. The woman was young, maybe in her mid-twenties, with long, blonde hair that was pulled back in a high ponytail, and she was wearing a black, knee-length skirt with a black suit jacket. Even in the dark, I could tell she was beautiful. The guy next to her was twice her size and looked like he'd just crawled out of a fucking dumpster, so I couldn't exactly blame her for being scared. I was just about to approach them when the guy reached out, jerked her purse out of her hand, and took off running. Without even thinking, I started chasing after him. He was fast, *really fast*. As I raced behind him, I was worried that I might not be able to catch up to him, especially since I was exhausted. But as soon as my adrenaline kicked in, I got close enough to lunge towards him. With a hard thud, I tackled him to the ground and used my weight to keep him in place. Once he'd recovered from the impact, he started thrashing around, trying with all his might to free himself from my grasp. Unfortunately for him, there was no way in hell I was gonna let him go. I yanked his arm behind his back, pinning him to the ground, then said, "Knock it off before I put a fucking bullet in you."

"What the hell are you doing?" he barked as he tried to buck me off him. "Get the fuck off me!"

Careful to keep it out of sight, I took my gun from the holster and shoved it into his side. "Not going to say it again, asshole."

"Whoa, man!" He stilled as he said, "I wasn't gonna hurt 'er. I just needed a few bucks. I'm jonesing something awful and need a fix."

"So, you just figured you'd steal a lady's purse? Damn." My patience was wearing thin. "You're a real piece of shit," I growled.

"Done told you. I wasn't gonna hurt 'er," he whined. "Just let me go and I'll get gone."

"I'm thinking that's not a good idea." I pulled his arm back even further, causing him to cry out. "I'm thinking you'll just do this shit again, and that doesn't work for me."

"No, man. I learned my lesson. I ain't gonna do it again. I swear it."

"You better mean that." I jabbed the barrel of my pistol into his side as I warned, "'Cause if you do … I'll find out and I'll come for you."

I picked up the woman's purse, then eased off him, making sure to grind my knee into his back. He managed to get up, and after giving me the once over, he scurried off. Once he was out of sight, I turned and headed back towards the young woman. When I got over to her, I handed her the purse and asked, "You okay?"

Her voice trembled as she replied, "Yes, I think so."

"Good. I was worried he might've hurt you." I expected her to say something more, but she just stood there staring at me with a stunned look. "You sure you're okay?"

"I'm a little shaken up, that's all."

"I imagine you are."

"I don't know what I was thinking." She dropped her head into her hands and groaned. "I should've known Haley wouldn't show."

"Haley?"

"She's one of the pharmaceutical sales reps at MBC Pharmaceuticals. We were supposed to meet at Morgan's for dinner, but she didn't show." She motioned her hand over to the back lot and continued, "Since I was parked close by, I thought I'd be okay, but then, that guy came out of nowhere."

"It's not your fault. Just need to be a little more careful at this time of night."

"I know. It was a stupid move. I don't know what I would've done if you hadn't come along." She looked up at me with those beautiful eyes, and I was done. "Thank you so much for helping me like you did."

"No need to thank me. Happy to help."

"Well, I really appreciate it." A light blush crossed her face as she asked, "If it's not too much to ask, would you mind walking me over to my car?"

"I'd be glad to."

As we started towards her car, she turned to me and said, "By the way, my name is Samantha Travers."

Samantha Travers. I repeated her name in my head, committing it to memory.

"Nice to meet you, Samantha. I'm Gus." When we

reached her car, I waited for her to unlock the door and get inside. "Be careful heading home."

"I will. Thanks again." I nodded and turned to leave. I'd only taken a few steps when I heard her call out to me. "Gus?"

There was something about the way she said my name that made my chest tighten. "Yeah?"

"Will I see you again?"

"You can count on it."

A smile crossed her face as she closed her door and started the engine. It was the kind of smile that let me know that she was interested, and I couldn't deny that I felt the same way.

SAMANTHA

"I just feel terrible," Haley complained. "I meant to call you to let you know that I couldn't make it, but it must've slipped my mind."

She'd called me into her office to apologize for being a no-show the night before. After hearing about what had happened with me, she was even more regretful. I'd been interning under Haley for the past couple of months, and things had been going really well. I didn't want anything to jeopardize my chance to land a job there, so I decided not to make a big deal of it. "It's okay. Things happen."

"It's not okay. You could've been hurt."

"Yes, but I'm perfectly fine."

She leaned forward and placed her elbows on her desk as she continued, "You watch the news. It seems like every night someone has been shot or raped. To think could've happened to you and it would've been all my fault!"

"Don't be silly. It wouldn't have been your fault." Haley had a flare for the dramatic and today was no different. I tried to settle her down by saying, "Besides, this man, Gus, was there to make sure nothing happened."

"Yes. Thank goodness for that!" A mischievous smile crossed Haley's face as she said, "Sooo …. Tell me more about this Gus fella. Was he hot?"

"Umm…Yeah, he was very hot. He was tall and muscular with dark hair and dark eyes."

"Ooo … Tall, dark, and handsome." She smiled. "I like it."

"I did, too." I could feel the warmth rush to my face as I thought back to the way he took charge of the situation and tackled that awful man to the ground like it was nothing. With his tattoos and thick beard, one might've thought I'd simply traded one bad guy for another, but that wasn't the case. There was something about him that made me feel safe and protected, something more than the fact that he'd rescued me. "He was a little rough around the edges, but in a good way … a very good way. I'd never met anyone like him before. Gus had this confidence that just radiated off him."

"And he just appeared out of nowhere?"

"Pretty much."

"Maybe he's some kind of superhero or something," she teased.

"I highly doubt that, but he definitely saved the day."

As she looked towards the doorway, her eyes grew wide. "You said the guy had dark hair and dark eyes. Did he, um, have a beard?"

"*Yes*."

"Was he wearing one of those motorcycle vests and boots?"

"Umm … yeah. I think so."

Haley was still looking over at the doorway as she continued with the questions, "And did he have tattoos?"

"Yes?" Curious to see what had her so enthralled, I turned to look behind me as I asked, "How did …?"

I didn't finish the question. I couldn't. My mind went completely blank when I noticed Gus walking in our direction, wearing jeans and a leather vest. He sure didn't look like the other men in our office—and I liked it. Different looked good on him. So good, if fact, I couldn't take my eyes off of him as he approached the doorway. "Hey."

"Hey." His eyes met mine as he said, "I thought I'd stop by to make sure you were okay."

"That's so sweet of you." I smiled as I stood up and walked over to him. "But, you didn't have to. I'm fine."

"I know I didn't have to." A sexy smirk crossed Gus's face as he said, "I wanted to."

Haley came up beside us and batted her long eyelashes as she purred, "Sam was just telling me how you came to her rescue last night. You're quite the hero."

"I'm far from a hero," he scoffed. "Just doing what I could to help."

"I'm Haley, by the way." She was practically drooling as she added, "Samantha and I work together."

He glanced over in her direction just long enough to say, "Nice to meet you. You mind if I have a moment with Samantha?"

"Oh, uh … sure," she stammered from the rejection. "I'll just go grab myself a cup of coffee."

Once she'd left the room, he looked back over to me and asked, "You got plans for tonight?"

"Um. No, not that I can think of."

"You wanna grab a burger or something after work?"

Trying not to act too eager, I forced myself to take a breath before I answered, "Sure. I could do that."

"What time do you get off?"

"Five o'clock."

"Great. I'll be here at five to pick you up."

I was dressed in a pair of slacks and a white dress blouse, not the kind of thing I would normally wear on a date, so I asked, "Umm ... could we make it five-thirty or six, and you pick me up at my place?"

"Absolutely. Just need your address."

"Okay." I grabbed a post-it note off of Haley's desk and wrote down my address. "Here ya go."

As Gus took the paper from my hand, he said, "Gonna be on my Harley, so wear jeans and boots if you have them."

"Your Harley? You mean a Harley motorcycle?"

His lips curled into the sexiest smile I'd ever seen. "You gonna be all right with that?"

"I've never ridden a motorcycle before."

Still smiling, he replied, "That didn't answer my question, Ms. Travers."

"Yes, I'm good with it."

"Great. I'll see you at six."

And just like that, he was gone. I probably would've spiraled into a fit of uncertainty about my impending date, but I had four appointments scheduled before noon and three after. I was already running late, so I rushed to my office, grabbed my things, and got out to my car before I got even more behind. I spent the entire day bouncing from one doctor's office to the next, so I didn't have time to dwell on my doubts about going on a date with a complete stranger and riding on a motorcycle for the first time. That freak-out came five minutes before he was supposed to arrive at my apartment. My heart was pounding in my chest and my palms were sweating as I looked at myself in the mirror. I took a couple of deep, cleansing breaths, but just as my nerves were starting to settle, I heard a knock at the door. I wiped my palms on my jeans, then made my way over to the door and slowly eased it open. When I saw Gus standing there looking all kinds of sexy in his jeans and leather jacket, my nerves kicked into high gear. Trying to pull it together, I forced a smile and said, "Hey. Come on in. I just need to grab my things."

"Take your time." Gus stepped inside my apartment and took a quick look around. "You've got a nice place."

"Thanks." I grabbed my purse and jacket off the sofa, then walked back over to him. "I'm ready when you are."

His expression grew soft as he said, "You look beautiful."

"Thank you. You look really nice, too."

Once we were downstairs and I spotted his big, black motorcycle parked next to the curb, I started to feel a little apprehensive. Sensing my unease, Gus stepped towards me and smiled. "Don't worry. There's nothing to it."

Minutes later, my arms were wrapped tightly around his waist, and we were weaving in and out of traffic. To my surprise, I actually loved being on the back of his bike, feeling the wind in my face and hearing the sounds of the city roaring in my ears. It didn't hurt that it gave me an excuse to be close to Gus. I loved his scent—a hint of cologne mixed with leather and smoke, and I loved how he appeared to be so confident and self-assured. It made me feel safe, like he was in complete control, and I was just there to enjoy the ride.

Just as we were leaving the city limits, Gus turned down an old, side road that led up to a small, crowded café. As we got off the bike and started inside, he smiled and said, "I know it doesn't look like much, but they have incredible burgers."

"Great. I can't wait to try one." He opened the front door and waited as I walked in ahead of him. As soon as I smelled the delectable scent of home-cooking, I immediately understood why the place was so packed. Gus reached for my hand and led me over to one of the empty booths in the back. Once we were seated, I told him, "It smells incredible."

"It tastes even better." He took a quick glance around, studying the old, rustic farm equipment and photographs on the walls before saying, "The club's going to open up a diner like this close to Beale Street, but instead of the old south, ours will have a Memphis blues theme to it."

I was about to ask what he was talking about when the waitress came over to take our order. After handing it into the kitchen, she returned with our tea and placed them on the table. I took a quick sip, then turned to Gus and said, "I'm not sure I know what you mean by the club."

"Yeah, I guess I should take a minute to explain that." For the next half-hour, he explained how the club was much more than a group of men who rode motorcycles and worked together, and that they were a family who lived and died for each other. I'd heard of clubs like his and knew some were decent, while others were bad, really bad, but I'd never actually met anyone who belonged to one, much less ran one. I didn't know what it meant to be a president of an MC, but it was clear that Gus took great pride in his position. He practically beamed as he told me how he'd been sent to Memphis to start up this new chapter of Satan's Fury, describing the progress they'd made. "The clubhouse is almost done, so now we can start moving in there and focus on getting the restaurant up and going."

"That sounds like a lot of work."

"It is, but it'll be worth it when we're finished." He took a sip of his drink before asking, "What about you? What's your story?"

"My story isn't nearly as exciting as yours," I admitted. "I grew up here in Memphis. I recently graduated from the U of M, and now I'm interning at MBC Pharmaceuticals. I'm hoping to start working for them full-time this summer."

"And your family?"

"I have one older brother, Thomas. He lives in South Carolina now, so I don't get to see him very often. And my parents … they can be a little much at times."

"How so?"

I didn't want to bore Gus with all the petty details of my controlled life, so I simply said, "Let's just say, my father is in politics, and my mother does her best to portray herself as the perfect, doting wife. She's quite the little socialite. Always doing community service projects and rubbing noses with the city's finest. You know how it is."

"No, I'm afraid I don't." He smiled as he used my own words against me. "But, it sounds like a lot of work."

"Yes, it is." I rolled my eyes, then continued, "Life

under the microscope is definitely not for the faint of heart. It's one of the reasons why I decided to go into a completely different line of work."

"Can't say I blame you there." He paused for a moment, then asked, "Since you grew up in the area, maybe you could give me some insight into a few things."

"Such as?"

"Okay. What's with all the bottles in the trees?"

"Oh, that's an old southern tradition. My grandmother once told me that people used to hang them to ward off evil spirits. They'd say that the spirits would be attracted to the sound of the bottles clinking together and end up getting trapped inside."

"Hmm. Not at all what I thought." He paused for a minute, then said, "I think I'm getting the hang of some of the southern phrases like fixin', over yonder, and blowin' up a storm, but there's one I'm still not sure about."

"Which one?"

"When women say *bless your heart*. That has more than one meaning, right?"

I couldn't help but laugh as I answered, "Yes. It has all kinds of meanings. It just depends on the situation."

"Not sure I'm following ya."

"Okay. It can be used to show genuine concern, like 'I'm so sorry to hear you aren't feeling well, and you have a fever, too? Oh, bless your heart'. And it can also be used to soften the blow of an insult, like 'that poor fella doesn't have the sense God gave a goose. *Bless his heart.*'" I smiled as I told him, "You just pay attention to the tone."

He chuckled as he said, "Now, that's just not right."

We talked nonstop through dinner, sharing stories about our pasts and hopes for the future. It seemed strange that two people from two completely different worlds could have so much to talk about. I was having a great time being there with him and was disappointed when he glanced around the empty restaurant and said, "I guess we better get going before they run us out of here."

I followed him out to the parking lot, and we were both silent as he helped me on the bike. Before I had a chance to say something cute or flirty, he started the engine and we were on our way back to my place. It seemed like we'd only been riding for a few minutes when Gus pulled up to the curb at my apartment and parked. I carefully eased off his bike and waited as he did the same. Once we'd both removed our helmets, I smiled and said, "I had a really good time tonight. Maybe we can do it again sometime."

He eased over to me. "You got plans for the weekend?"

Gus stood just inches away, and the way he looked at me made every nerve in my body tingle with lustful desire that I almost forgot to answer his question. "Um … no. I don't have any plans."

"You do now." Before I had time to think, he'd placed his hands on my waist and pulled me against his chest. My heart started to race with anticipation as he lowered his mouth to mine and kissed me. His lips were soft and warm, and suddenly, I was leaning right into him. It was clear that he was no *Prince Charming*. There was no white horse. No castle on the hill. He was rough, tough, and sexy as hell—and oh my, the man could kiss. His arms wound tightened around me, inching me even closer as his tongue found its way into my mouth. I was holding on by a thread, and just as I was becoming completely lost in his touch, he pulled back, quickly breaking our embrace.

His dark eyes danced with lust as they locked on mine. As he handed me his card, he said, "Friday night at seven. If something comes up, just call me at that number."

"Okay."

He leaned in for one last, brief kiss, then said, "Good night, Samantha."

"Good night, Gus." I turned and headed up the front steps. Just before I went inside, I turned back to him and said, "I'll see you Friday night."

"Looking forward to it."

As I opened the door, I couldn't help but smile. I knew it was just one date, one simple dinner, and yet, I knew it was so much more.

It was the beginning—*our beginning.*

GUS

On the day of Daisy Mae's grand opening, only a handful of customers had shown up, and the weeks that followed weren't much better. I was beginning to think that opening the diner was a mistake, but then, things took am impressive turn. For one reason or another, customers started streaming in, and it wasn't long before we were packed from open to close. Our hard work was finally starting to pay off. The renovations to the clubhouse were complete, the diner was thriving, and we'd even taken on a handful of new prospects and were looking at the Lost Knights MC as a possible patch over club. They were a small club with only twenty members, but they showed great potential—the kind of potential they'd need in order to be patched in as members of Fury. I was feeling pretty good about things, so I decided to take Samantha somewhere special to celebrate. I wanted it to be a surprise, so I didn't give her much to go on—just the time when I was coming by to pick her up and that she should wear something comfortable. Of course, that didn't set well with her. She was one of those women who liked to be prepared, so when I knocked on her door, I wasn't surprised when she came out of her apartment with a large duffle bag in her hand.

"You planning on moving in?" I cocked my eyebrow as I teased, "We've only been seeing each other for a few weeks, but I'm good with it. It would be nice to wake up with you next to me every morning."

"Umm, no." Samantha gave me one of her looks as she answered, "I brought the bag because somebody wouldn't tell me what we were doing tonight."

I didn't understand her concern. She looked absolutely stunning in her jean-shorts and sandals, so I asked, "Did you or did you not hear me say to wear something comfortable?"

"Yes, but that's all you would tell me. Comfortable could mean flip-flops and shorts or a t-shirt and pajama pants, or jeans and—"

"Okay. Okay," I interrupted. "I get it. I'll try to be more specific next time."

A satisfied smirk crossed her face as she asked, "Does that mean you're going to tell me where we're going tonight?"

"Nope." I took a hold of her duffle-bag and started walking towards the elevator. "Come on, beautiful. The clock's a-ticking. We don't want to be late."

"Late for what?"

"You'll see." As soon as the elevator doors closed, I reached for her waist and pulled her close. "You know, it never fails."

"What?"

"Just seeing you makes my day."

Samantha's expression softened as she wrapped her arms around my neck. "Well, in case you didn't know, you do the same thing to me."

"You gotta stop doing that."

"Doing what?"

"Stealing my compliments," I teased.

"I don't steal your compliments!" She paused for a moment, then added, "Well, I do, but only if I mean it."

"Um-hmm." I placed my hands on her hips and inched her even closer. "I know something you could do to make it up to me?"

"Oh, really?" She smiled. "And what's that?"

I leaned towards her, pressing my mouth against hers, and kissed her long and hard. Like so many times before, her body melted into mine, making me ache for more. I didn't understand how one woman could turn me inside out the way she did. Her touch, her scent ... everything about Samantha made me lose all sense of control. She shifted her stance causing the rigid length of my erection to press against her. A light moan rippled through her chest, and I was suddenly torn between taking her right there in the elevator or carrying her back upstairs and throwing her on the bed. Sadly, neither was an option—at least not for the time being. I had special plans for her tonight, so before we got any more carried away, I took a step back and released her from our embrace. "Damn woman. You keep kissing me like that, and we'll never make it out of this elevator."

A mischievous look danced in her eyes. "I'd be okay with that."

"I would be, too, but if we don't get moving, we're going to be late." I leaned forward and kissed her on the

25

temple. "But, I have every intention of picking up from here when we get back later tonight."

Before she could respond, the elevator doors opened, and I led her out to the SUV. After I put her duffle-bag in the backseat, we got inside, then I drove us over to the Shelby Farms Park. By the time we arrived at the park it was well after dark, and people had already started to claim their spots on the lawn. Once we got out of the SUV, I went straight to the back and grabbed blanket and the picnic basket of food that Louise had fixed for us. Samantha came over to me with a surprised look and asked, "What's all this?"

"You'll see."

While we made our way towards the crowd, Samantha noticed the large movie screen tucked in the corner by the trees and smiled. "A movie night at the park?"

"Yeah, I heard some folks talking about it down at the diner. I thought it might be something cool to try."

"It's very cool." She followed me over to an open area towards the back and helped me spread out the blanket. As we sat down, she gave me a sly smirk. "Look at you being all romantic."

Using my best, fake southern accent, I told her, "I'm just gettin' started, darlin'."

After we finished eating, Samantha curled up next to me, and just as I hoped, she loved the movie. I, on the other hand, had no idea what it was even about. I was too busy watching her to keep up with what was going on. I couldn't seem to help myself. With every moment I spent with Samantha, I found another reason to fall for her—the way her nose crinkled when she laughed, the sound of her voice when she said my name, or the softness of her lips when they were pressed against mine. I never imagined that I'd ever find someone who got to me the way she did, but damn. Samantha was everything I'd always wanted and more. She had me thinking about us having a future together, and the more I thought about it, the more I liked the idea.

When the movie was over, we collected our things and headed back to the truck. Samantha was practically beaming as she said, "I can't remember enjoying a movie as much as I did tonight."

"Good. I'm glad you liked it."

As she got inside the truck, she asked, "So, where to now?"

"That's up to you. We could head over to the clubhouse and have a couple of drinks or we could go back to your place and pick up where we left off in the elevator."

"Hmmm." A smirk crossed her face as she answered, "I guess if I have to decide … I'd have to go with …. picking up where we left off in the elevator."

As I pulled out of the parking lot, I told her, "I was hoping you'd say that."

Not wanting to waste another second, I pressed my foot against the accelerator and sped towards her apartment. Samantha rushed over to the elevator and she glanced over to me with lust-filled eyes as she pressed the button. Anticipation crackled around us as we waited there together, and a relieved smile crossed her face when the doors finally opened. She stepped inside and watched with bated breath as I took a charging step forward, pinning her back against the wall. I looked down at Samantha and watched the rise and fall of her chest as she panted with need. Her eyes darkened as her gaze drifted to my lips. When she couldn't stand it a moment longer, her fingers dove into my hair, and she pulled me towards her, crashing her mouth against mine in a hungry kiss. The kiss quickly became heated, making my cock throb with need.

"Dammit, woman. You're killing me," I told her as my hand dropped to her shorts. With a quick twist, I undid the first couple of buttons, then slipped my hand down her shorts. A light hiss escaped her lungs when I eased the lining of her lace panties to the side and grazed her center with the tips of my fingers—my already hard cock pulsed against my zipper when I found she was already soaked. "Damn. You're so fuckin' wet for me."

She gasped as I used my free hand to lower her shirt just enough to reveal her perfectly round breasts. With her eyes on mine, I lowered my mouth and began swirling my tongue around her nipple. Her head fell back as she moaned, "Oh God."

I nipped and sucked, relishing the sounds of her little moans and whimpers as I teased her with my tongue and my teeth. I cursed when the elevator doors opened. After I removed my hand from her shorts and she adjusted her tank top, I followed her inside the apartment. As soon as Samantha closed the door and tossed her things on the counter, she unbuttoned her shorts and let them fall to the floor. When I started towards her, she took several steps back, watching me like I was a starved predator as she bumped into the kitchen table. "You have any idea how bad I want you right now?"

"Um-hmm." She purred. "Just as much as I want you."

I lowered my hands to her hips and reached for her lace panties, sliding them down her long, lean legs. Desire flashed through her eyes as I lifted her up, then guided her to lay back on the table. I was so thirsty for her that I could barely think as I eased her legs over my shoulders and lowered my mouth between her thighs. She inhaled a deep breath when the bristles of my beard brushed against her soft skin, her back arching off the table as my tongue skimmed across her smooth center. I spread her trembling legs wider, and a needful moan echoed through the room as I slid my tongue between her folds. "Damn, baby. You taste like fucking heaven."

Samantha's breath became uneven and hitched as I slipped my finger deep inside her. Focused and unrelenting, I teased her g-spot with a slow and steady rhythm. Her hips inched forward as she tensed around me and goosebumps prickled across her skin. Loving how her beautiful body responded to my touch, I continued grazing and teasing her clit with my tongue, tormenting her as she writhed beneath me. Overcome by her impending release, her hips lifted up from the table, begging for me to give her more. I instantly drove another finger deep inside her while I played with her clit using the pad of my thumb until she got exactly what she needed.

Her head thrashed back as she gasped, "Yes!"

"That's it, baby."

I slid my tongue over her as I continued moving my fingers inside her, tormenting that spot that was driving her to the edge. Adding more pressure, I demanded, "Come for me."

That's all it took. While muttering my name incoherently, she submitted to her release and clamped down around my fingers. Damn. Nothing turned me on more than watching her come undone. I couldn't wait a moment longer. I had to be inside her. She was still in the throes of her release when I got undressed and rolled on a condom. Her eyes locked on mine as I slipped my hands under her ass and pulled her to the edge of the table. *Fuck.* She looked so damn beautiful sprawled out on that table, bare and waiting for me with that wanton look in her eyes. I couldn't imagine wanting her more.

As I brushed my throbbing cock against her slick center and nearly lost it. Inhaling a deep breath, I tried to calm the storm of need that was raging inside of me, but my woman was eager for more. Unable to wait a moment longer, she wrapped her legs around me and forced me deep inside. I froze. She felt too fucking good. As I slowly withdrew, I looked down at her and asked, "You like having my cock inside you?"

She managed a slight nod as she muttered, "God, yes!"

A slight hiss slipped through her teeth as I drove into her again and again—each time a bit faster and more unforgiving. Her heels dug into my back and she shouted, "Gus!"

As much as I loved having her this way, I wanted more. I needed to feel her, touch every inch of her gorgeous body, so I lowered her legs to my waist and carefully lifted her from the table. With my cock still buried deep inside her, I carried her over to the sofa and lowered us down onto the cushions, letting Samantha's knees straddle me. I dropped my hands to her waist and started guiding her over my cock in an unforgiving rhythm. She placed her hands on my shoulders, trying to steady herself as she shouted, "Gus!"

There was something about hearing her call out my

name that sent an intense heat coursing through my body. I burned for her, every fucking inch of me was consumed by my need for this woman, and I knew I'd never feel this way for anyone else. Samantha would be mine—all mine, heart and soul. Shifting her hips upward, she continued to gyrate against me, grinding her warm, wet pussy over my cock. When I rocked against her, I could feel her muscles contracting all around me as her second orgasm started to take hold. My body grew rigid as my release inched its way through me. Her head fell back as she cried out, "Oh my God, Gus! *I'm coming!*"

I fisted my hand in her long hair, giving it a gentle tug, as I thrust forward, driving inside her once again. She was so fucking hot, so tight, and it was all too much. Damn. I couldn't imagine a better feeling. I drew back and slammed into her again, taking her harder and deeper.

"Fuckkk!" I shouted out as my throbbing cock demanded its release. My fingers dug into her hips as I guided her forward in a feverish rhythm until I came deep inside of her. We both stilled, fighting to catch our breath, and after several moments, our heartbeats began to slow.

"Woman, you're gonna be the death of me."

"Oh, really?" Looking slightly dazed and completely sated, a sexy smile spread across her gorgeous face. "You complaining?"

"Umm … *Hell, no.*" I glanced down at my cock still buried deep inside her as I said, "I can't think of a better way to go."

"Neither can I." She placed the palms of her hands on my face as she said, "I love you."

"Good thing you do, cause you're stuck with me."

31

"I'm good with that." She pressed her lips to mine, then added, "I kind of like having you around."

"Kinda?" Before I could continue, my cell started to ring. Knowing the boys wouldn't call unless there was a problem, I lifted her off of me and said, "Sorry, baby. I gotta get that."

Once I'd lowered her to the sofa, I got up and pulled off my condom, quickly tossing into the trash before grabbed my phone. "Yeah?"

"The Ravens made their move," T-Bone announced. "Gonna need you to get back to the clubhouse."

The Ravens were a small, local gang who'd been making their presence known over the past couple of weeks. At first it was just idle threats and graffiti, but they were steadily stepping up their game. It was to be expected. The more it got out that a new MC was in town —especially one with the kind of reputation Satan's Fury carried—there would be those who'd try to take us down. It was up to me to make sure that shit didn't happen. The Ravens had no idea who they were fucking with. Even though we were still building our numbers, they were no match for us. "I'll be there in ten."

As much as I didn't want to leave Samantha, there wasn't a choice, so I threw on my clothes, kissed her goodbye, and headed out to my bike. When I got to the clubhouse, T-Bone was waiting for me at the front door. "What happened?"

"Widow was coming through town with a couple of the prospects when two black Audis came racing up beside them and started shooting. They shot Widow and Sprocket ..." His voice trailed off for a moment. "They didn't make it, Gus."

"Fuck!" I spat. "You sure it was the Ravens?"

"Yeah," he growled. "The motherfuckers were sporting their colors."

"We end this shit, now."

"I'm with you, brother. Got any idea on how we're gonna make that happen?"

"It's time to see if the Lost Knights really have what it takes to wear the Fury name." As I reached into my pocket for my phone, I continued, "If they're half the club they claim to be, then we'll have all the manpower we need to take those motherfuckers down."

Rage surged through me as I dialed Brewer's number, the Lost Knight's president. I'd barely gotten out all the details of what had happened when he said, "We're on our way."

Fifteen minutes later, the Lost Knights came rolling into our parking lot, ready and eager to prove themselves. I headed over to Brewer, and as I shook his hand, I told him, "Appreciate you boys coming to give us a hand."

"Don't mention it." He shook his head, as he said, "The Ravens fucked up tonight."

"That they did." I couldn't hold back my anger as I said, "They came looking for trouble and they fucking found it. We're going to burn those motherfuckers to the ground."

"We're here for you, brother. Just tell me what you need us to do."

"Appreciate that." Knowing we'd already lost two brothers, I warned, "We need to be smart about this. Gotta get in and get out."

"Understood."

After laying out a plan, we loaded our ammunition in the back of my SUV and headed over towards the Raven's warehouse. Under the circumstances, we had to act fast and catch them off guard, so we didn't have the luxury of setting up surveillance and monitoring them for weeks on end. Once we got close to their warehouse, we drove up into an abandoned lot and got out, quickly surrounding their compound. Armed and ready, we searched for the best entry point. When we found a backdoor open, Brewer and two of his men, Grinder and Rivet, followed Moose and me inside while T-Bone and Bane monitored the front. As I'd hoped, the Ravens were a bunch of fucking dumbasses with no fucking security and had no idea that we'd just entered the room. Six guys were sitting around a table playing cards, three were on a sofa just shooting the shit, and others were huddled around a couple of cars they'd been working on. As soon as they saw us, they started scampering for their weapons, but it was too late. Gun fire rang out through the entire warehouse, and one by one, their lifeless bodies fell to the floor. Once we'd taken them all out, we burned their warehouse to the ground, and there was nothing left of the Ravens.

While the war over the territory was far from over, we'd won our battle over the Ravens. I was grateful that the Lost Knights had come through for us, and I had no doubt that Saul and the others would agree that they'd proven themselves worthy of being patched over. The city of Memphis would soon learn that Satan's Fury MC was here to stay, and if I had anything to say about it, the territory would be ours to reign supreme above all others.

SAMANTHA

"*L*auren and I are gonna head down to Morgan's after work to grab a few drinks," Haley announced as she stepped into my office. "You should come along. Help us shake off the horrendous week."

"I wish I could, but …"

"Let me guess," she answered with a smile. "You've got plans with Mr. Wonderful tonight."

"That, I do." Over the past few months, we'd been spending a lot of time together, especially on the weekends, but since the night he'd rushed out of my apartment, I'd only seen him once and that was only for a couple of hours. Something was going on with the club—something he couldn't tell me about. Whenever I asked him about it, he'd tell me that he was doing everything in his power to resolve it before things got out of hand. I wanted desperately to know more, but he'd made it clear that there were aspects of the club that I simply wasn't privy to. I tried not to let it hurt my feelings, but it hadn't been easy. I wanted to help or at the very least be there for him, but he simply wouldn't allow it. I did my best to hide my concern as I feigned a smile and said, "The guys are having a birthday party for Rayne tonight, and Gus asked me to come."

As she stepped into my office she asked, "So, things are going good with you two?"

"Yeah. Things are better than good." I could feel myself smiling as I added, "We're still figuring things out and all that."

"I totally understand." Haley's tone changed as she asked, "Have you thought about what you'll do if you get transferred to the Nashville office?"

"Yes and no. I was waiting to see if I actually got the position before I started worrying about how it would affect things with us."

"So, you haven't even mentioned it to him?"

"No, not really."

"Sam, if things are going as well as you say they are, then you need to talk to him. It's only fair."

"You're right." A nervous feeling washed over me. "I will tonight."

"Good." As she turned to leave, she gave me a half-smile and said, "If you get done with the party early, give me a call. Maybe you can meet up with us after."

"Sounds good. I'll definitely do that."

"Great." With a quick wave, she turned and walked out of my office. "Catch ya later, alligator."

Once she was gone, I turned my attention back to my weekly reports, so I could leave on time. Gus was expecting me at the clubhouse at six and I still needed to run by the apartment to change and grab Rayne's birthday gift. As soon as I finished my report, I emailed it to my advisor, then shut down my computer and gathered my things. When I got out to my car, I was relieved to see that I was actually ahead of schedule. If I played it right, I could be there well before the party started, and I might even get a few minutes alone with Gus. Unfortunately, everything usually took me longer than I planned, so by the time I arrived at the clubhouse, everyone was already gathered in the family room. Balloons were strung in every corner and presents were piled high on the front table, and Rayne couldn't have looked more excited as she sat perched on Louise's hip. As I walked over to place my gift with the others, I smiled at Rayne and said, "Happy birthday, sweet girl."

"I'm t'ree," she boasted as she tried to hold up three fingers. "I'm dis many."

"I know you are! You're such a big girl, now."

"She likes to think so," Louise scoffed.

Rayne leaned forward and tried to grab one of the presents as she stated, "Mine."

"Not yet, Rayne."

"Mine, Momma."

"I know they're yours, baby, but it's not time to open presents yet." Louise looked over to me and sighed. "I blame her father for this. He spoils her like crazy."

I really liked Louise. She was beautiful with shoulder-length hair and a killer figure, but she never used her looks to get what she wanted. She was too smart, too strong-willed, for that. When Louise set her mind to something, she made it happen, and everyone who knew her respected her for it. I smiled as I told her, "Daddy's have a way of spoiling their little girls. I know my father always did me."

"Mine spoiled me, too, but Moose is going to make her absolutely rotten." She motioned her hand towards the table of gifts. "Most of these are from him, and all she'll care about are the boxes and the balloons."

When Rayne reached for one of the balloons and fisted it in her little hand, I giggled as I said, "You might be right about that."

We were both laughing when Gus came up behind me and wrapped his arms around my waist, easing me back against his chest as he whispered, "Hey there, beautiful."

The sound of his voice sent a delicious chill down my spine, causing my knees to tremble as I leaned against him. "Hey, I'm sorry I was late."

"You're right on time." He lowered his mouth to my neck, softly kissing me before turning me around to face him. "Glad you could make it."

"I wouldn't miss it." I took a quick glance around the room, and I was surprised by how many brothers were gathered in the family room. When Gus first brought me to the clubhouse, there were only six brothers and two prospects. But now, they were making plans to patch over the members of the Lost Knights, and they'd also enlisted four new prospects. I couldn't help but noticed that one of them wasn't in the family room and neither was Widow. "Looks like you have a couple who are even later than me. Are Widow and Reeves working at the diner?"

"No. They aren't working at the diner." There was no hiding the anguish in his eyes as he continued, "They ran into a little trouble. I'll tell you about it later."

"Oh. Okay." That left me curious and concerned but knew better than to push. I'd noticed several men in the back corner wearing Satan's Fury cuts, but I'd never seen them before. I looked over in their direction as I asked him, "Who are the new guys?"

"Oh, that's Saul. He's the president of the Washington chapter, and the other two are a couple of brothers he brought along with him."

"They're from your old club?"

"Yeah. Same club. Different state." I could tell he was holding something back when he added, "They came down to help me get a few things sorted, but they'll be heading back in the morning."

After hearing that there had been some trouble with Widow and Reeves, I couldn't help but wonder if that's why they'd come to Memphis. I knew I was pushing it, but I had to ask, "Is everything okay?"

"It is now." He reached for my hand. "Let's go grab a beer, and then, I'll take you over and introduce you."

"Okay."

I was a little nervous about meeting people who'd had such an important impact in his life, but I quickly learned I had nothing to worry about. They were just as kind and loyal as Gus's other brothers, and they treated me like they'd known me for years. It was easy to see why Gus loved being with them like he did. Even though they weren't blood relatives, they truly were like his family, and I found myself wondering if they could be mine as well.

Dinner was almost ready, so we all moved into the family room to watch Rayne open her presents. By the time she was done, it looked like a toy store had exploded in the family room. I couldn't help but laugh when I glanced over at Rayne and watched her play with all the empty boxes. She was building a small tower when I leaned over to Louise and whispered, "You were right about the boxes."

Nodding, she replied, "At least now I know what to get her for Christmas!"

"That you do!"

By the time dinner was ready, Rayne was starting to tucker out, so Louise had one of the girls carry her back to Gus's room and put her down for bed. Once we'd brought all the food out from the kitchen, we gathered around the table and made our plates. We all started eating, and it wasn't long before the guys started goofing around, poking fun at one another. When the topic of conversations turned to old flames, Bane looked at T-Bone and asked, "What about that chick who wanted to marry your sorry ass? She was hot as fuck. I can't believe you passed that up."

"She might've been hot, but that chick was three shades of fucked up." T-Bone looked horrified as he continued, "She had a list of rules for me on the refrigerator ... and she smelled my clothes, especially my underwear." He cocked his eyebrow and nodded. "Yeah ... my *fucking underwear*, and she followed me around like some kind of goddamn stalker. Calling at all times of the damn night, over and over. But worst of all, she refused to give head. Said it wasn't hygienic."

When the laughter finally died down, Half-pint looked over to him and said, "My ex used to take pictures of me when I was sleeping. Used to creep me the fuck out."

"One of my exes used to spray her perfume in my bed. Guess she thought other chicks might smell it and hit the ground running, but it just ended up making me smell like a fucking pussy," Bane complained.

"Oh, hell. That's nothing. I was with this one girl who had a thing for feet, and … damn." Cyrus's face turned an odd shade of green as he told us, "Some of the shit she wanted to do. It just wasn't right."

The room exploded in laughter, but Cyrus was too lost in his thoughts to even care. The guys continued to tell stories and carry on until everyone had finished eating. We cleaned up the dishes, and everyone was talking amongst themselves in the kitchen when Gus leaned over to me and said, "I need to have a quick word with Saul, and then, I'll run you home."

"But, I drove here."

"In that case, I'll follow you home." He placed his hands on my hips and pulled me towards him as he said, "Unless you have a problem with me spending some time with my woman."

"No, I don't have a problem with that." I inched a little closer. "In fact, I was going to be a little disappointed if I didn't get a little alone time with you."

He leaned forward and kissed me on the forehead. As he turned to leave, he said, "Give me a minute … five at the most."

When he turned to leave, I headed over to the others to say my goodbyes. Louise and Moose thanked me for the gift I'd given Rayne, and then T-Bone and the others each took a moment to speak before they wandered over to the bar. I was about to head out to the parking lot when

I saw Gus walking in my direction. Just the sight of him got to me like no other man had before. He was just so damn handsome, so confident and self-assured, and the way he looked at me, like I was the most beautiful woman on the planet, made every nerve in my body long to be touched by him. As he made his way over to me, I smiled and said, "That was fast."

Gus wrapped his arms around me and lifted me in the air. "Told ya I just needed a minute."

"That, you did."

Then, he gave me a brief kiss and lowered my feet to the floor. Wasting no time, he took my hand and started for the door. "Let's get out of here."

Once he'd walked me over to my car and got me settled inside, he went over to his bike and followed me over to my apartment. We parked and headed inside and got on the elevator. The second the doors closed, we were on each other like two sex-crazed teenagers, kissing and pawing like there was no tomorrow. When the doors opened, Gus lifted me into his arms and carried me to my apartment door. Fumbling with the key, I finally unlocked it. When he carried me inside, I was surprised to find that my lights were on. Gus was about to lean in for another kiss, when I scooted out of his arms and stepped into the living room. As soon as I saw her, and noticed the expression on her face, my heart dropped to the pit of my stomach.

"Hello, Samantha Grace."

"*Mom* … Umm, what are you doing here?"

Her eyebrow was raised high in annoyance as she said, "If you had checked your cell phone, you'd know that I was coming."

"I'm sorry." Gus walked up next to me as I told her, "We were at a birthday party, and I—"

I'd never told her anything about who I'd been seeing, so I was surprised when she stood up and interrupted me by saying, "You must be Gus."

"I am."

"Well, it's nice to finally meet you." She extended her hand as she said, "I'm Elizabeth Travers. Samantha's mother."

As he shook her hand, he replied, "It's nice to meet you, too, Mrs. Travers. Samantha has told me a lot about you and your family."

"Well, that's nice to hear. Wish I could say the same about you." She was wearing one of her fitted blouses and a string of pearls along with black slacks and heels, but it wasn't what she was wearing that made her seem pretentious. It was the way she looked at him, and the tone she used when she spoke. Mom didn't have to say the words. She'd already made it clear that she didn't approve of Gus, and to top it off, she glanced over at me with one of her looks. I knew then I was in for it. Her focus was still on me while she told Gus, "Maybe we can rectify that in a bit when Samantha and I are *alone*. I'm sure we will have lots to talk about."

He seemed completely unfazed by her rude behavior as he answered, "I'm sure you will."

"Mom," I warned.

Before I could say anything more, Gus looked over to me and said, "I'm gonna get going."

"Wait. You don't have to leave." I glared over at my mother as I told him, "She won't be staying long."

"You need to spend some time with your mother,

Sam." He leaned towards me and kissed my cheek briefly before saying, "I'll check in with you tomorrow."

"Are you sure?"

"Positive. I wasn't able to stay long anyway."

"Okay." Disappointment washed over me as I followed him over to the door. Before he walked out, I whispered, "I'm sorry about this."

"Don't be." Gus kissed me one more time, then stepped into the hall. Before I closed the door, he called out to my mother, "It was nice meeting you, Mrs. Travers."

She didn't respond, which only aggravated me even more. Once he was gone, I stormed back into the living room and asked, "What the hell was that?"

"I was about to ask you the same," she snapped. "And watch your tone, young lady. I don't care how old you get, I am still your mother and I will not be disrespected."

"I'm not trying to be disrespectful, Mother." I took in a deep breath and crossed my arms as I told her. "I just want to know what you're doing here?"

"I came because I heard that my daughter had gotten herself a new boyfriend."

"And where did you hear that?"

"From Evan. Everyone informed us that he was the best campaign manager in the country, but when he alerted me that my daughter had gotten herself mixed up with some delinquent, I thought he'd made a terrible mistake. Then, lo and behold, I arrive only to find you here with him." She walked over to the window and watched Gus get on his motorcycle, then grumbled, "A biker, Samantha? How could you delve so low?"

"You're wrong about him, Mom. He's not a delinquent. He's a good man, and he's been very wonderful to me."

Her back was still turned away from me when I said, "I love him. I don't care if you approve of him or not."

"And your father? What about him? Do you care about him at all?"

"You know I do."

"Well, you certainly aren't acting like it." She turned to face me as she continued, "You know what becoming governor means to him. He's spent his entire life working for this chance, and how do you think he's going to feel when you're the one who takes it away from him."

"What are you talking about? I'm not taking anything away from him."

"Of course you are! When the media learns that their lead candidate … the man who has an impeccable record with not one single skeleton in his closet, has a daughter who is tangled up with some delinquent who belongs to one of the most dangerous biker clubs in the country, then your father's political career is over!" Her face flushed red as she continued her rant. "He's supposed to turn this state around and make it a safe, thriving place for the rich and the poor. How's he supposed to do that when his own daughter is running around with criminals?"

"Just because he's in a motorcycle club, that doesn't mean he's a criminal, Mother."

"No, but he is." With a huff, she stormed over to my coffee table and picked up a folder. As she thrust it in my direction, she spat, "See for yourself."

I opened the file and quickly scanned the first page. It was a record for an Augustus Peterson, born in Piedmont, Washington, in 1966. At first, I was thrown by the name Augustus Tanner, but when I got to the bottom of the page, I noticed a black and white photograph of Gus. I looked up at my mother as I asked, "What is this?"

"It's everything he could find on your new boyfriend. From the looks of it, he's been a very busy man."

"You had no right to do that!" I tossed the folder down on the coffee table in anger.

"Of course, I did! Your father's career is at stake!" She walked over to me and sighed. "You father has moved heaven and earth for you, Samantha ... giving you everything you could have ever wanted, including this apartment and that internship at MBC. Now, it's time for you to return the favor. End this thing with the biker before it's too late."

"I'm not ending things with him."

"I know you think you love him, but he's simply not the right man for you." She placed her hand on my face as she continued, "He can't give you the kind of life you deserve."

"He can and he will."

"I wish that were true, but it's not. You'll see that for yourself soon enough." She lowered her hand and let out a deep breath. "Your father had a meeting with a nice young man last week. His name is Denis Rayburn. He's a lawyer in Nashville, comes from a good family, and everyone thinks highly of him. We were thinking of having him come for dinner in a couple of weeks. You should come, especially considering your new position at work. You two would be in the same city."

"That's not going to happen."

"Just think about it." She picked up her purse and coat from the sofa, then added, "In fact, I want you to think about everything I've said tonight. Your family is counting on you to do the right thing."

With that, she turned and walked out. As soon as the door closed, I broke down in tears. I wasn't sure why I was crying. Maybe it was the fact that I was so angry about all the terrible things my mother said about Gus, or maybe it was because I knew she was right.

GUS

*S*amantha's body grew rigid as I began to thrust deeper, harder. Her snug pussy throbbed against me, weakening all of my restraint. When she showed up tonight in that tight, little, black dress and those fuck me heels, I knew exactly what she was up to. My little temptress wanted my attention, and by God, she fucking got it. I was done the second she walked into the room and I saw that spark of lust in her eyes, I was done. I tossed Samantha over my shoulder and carried her straight back to my room. I watched with bated breath as she slowly undressed and revealed her perfect curves, then I led her over to the bed. After I shed my clothes, I lowered myself down between her thighs and explored every inch of her body, making her come undone over and over again. Once I was inside her, I intended to go slow… wanting to savor every damn second, but she was so tight, so warm and wet. I couldn't hold back. I tightened my grip on her hair as I quickened my pace to a demanding rhythm. Her nails skated up my spine as her hips bucked against mine, meeting my every thrust with more force… more intensity. I could feel the pressure building in my cock as she constricted around me.

Her head reared back as she shouted, "Oh god, Gus!"

"Fuck," I groaned as she clamped down on me like a fucking vice. She panted wildly, moaning and clawing at my back as I plunged deeper. I knew she was close to the edge, unable to stop her impending release. I looked down at her, and my chest literally ached with emotion. This woman had a hold on me like I never thought possible. I lowered my mouth to her neck and whispered, "Mine."

"Yes!" she cried out in pleasure. The muscles in her body grew taut, then stilled as her orgasm took hold. I continued to drive into her, the sounds of my body pounding against hers echoed throughout the room and pushed me over the edge. My hands reached under her and lifted her ass off the bed as I drove into her one last time, submitting to my own tortured release.

Samantha's body fell limp under mine. I remained deeply seated inside her, not ready for the moment to end. I would miss nights like these if she decided to take that job in Nashville. I was surprised when she'd mentioned it earlier in the week, but knowing what it meant to her, I assured her that we'd make it work. That didn't mean I was happy about the idea of her being away from me. I rested my head on her chest and listened to her rapid heartbeat begin to steady. Samantha's breathing began to slow to a point that I thought she'd actually fallen asleep. I looked up at her and was surprised to see a sexy smile on her face. Settling myself alongside her, she slowly began to wiggle her way into the crook of my arm and rested her head down on my chest. I leaned over and kissed her on the temple. "You are really something, Samantha Travers."

"You are, too."

"There you go again … stealing my compliments," I joked.

"Well, they're good compliments. I can't seem to help myself." She giggled, and my heart nearly leapt out of my chest. "But, I have one you haven't used yet."

"Oh, really? What's that?"

She trailed the tips of her fingers across my chest as she whispered, "I love you more every minute of every day."

"You're right. I haven't used that one." I hadn't said those three little words to her yet. She knew I loved her. I showed her in every way I could, but clearly she needed to hear me say it. "But, that doesn't mean I don't love you, because I do. I think you know that."

"I do." She smiled and said, "Seems strange."

"What?"

"That we might not have met if that guy hadn't tried to steal my purse."

"It might've taken me a little longer, but I would've found you, Samantha. You were meant to be mine. I have no doubt about that."

The room fell silent for a moment, and then she glanced up at me and said, "I think we missed our dinner reservations."

"Yeah. I'd say I'm sorry, but that's on you."

"On me? How so?"

"You knew what would happen when I saw you in that dress."

"Are you saying I had ulterior motives for wearing that dress tonight?" she asked, feigning innocence.

"That's exactly what I'm saying." I looked down at her beautiful face. "You thinkin' I'm wrong?"

"Nope." She giggled. "Not at all."

"That's what I thought. You knew exactly what you were doing, so now, you have to decide what we're gonna do for dinner."

"How about a night in? We can order a pizza and watch a movie."

"Sounds like a plan to me."

After the club's encounter with the Ravens, we all struggled to come to terms with the loss of one of our brothers and a prospect—especially me. It was my job to keep my boys out of harm's way, and it gutted me that I'd failed them. Samantha knew something wasn't right, but she didn't push. While she was still learning the ins and outs of the club life, she understood that there were things that I simply couldn't, wouldn't share with her. Things were just starting to get settled down with the club when Sam mentioned a possible job transfer to Nashville. I had barely had a chance to wrap my head around the news when her mother showed up for an unexpected visit. I knew the moment we met that she wasn't happy about us being together. It wasn't like she tried to hide the fact, and even though Samantha tried to deny it, I knew it got to her. I wasn't blind. I could see the worry in her eyes, the wheels turning in her head whenever she was at the clubhouse, but I could also feel the love she felt for me whenever she was in my arms. Samantha and I were from two different worlds, traveling on two completely different paths, but something about us worked.

Once our pizza arrived, we made a make-shift picnic on the edge of the bed and started a movie. As Samantha took a bite of her pizza, she asked, "Do you think you'll ever get a place of your own like Moose and Louise?"

"Eventually. Right now, I need to be here so I can keep an eye on things."

"So, in a couple of months or a couple of years?"

"A year. Maybe a little less." Before I took a drink of my beer, I told her, "It just depends on how things play out."

"And what about kids?"

"What about 'em?"

She rolled her eyes. "Do you want any?"

"Yeah, sure. Just not right now." As I reached for another slice of pizza, I went on to say, "I've got too much on my plate to even consider taking on more. Maybe in a few years."

"Oh. Okay."

When her eyes skirted over to the floor, I knew something was up. "You got something on your mind?"

"I'm just trying to see where you stand, I guess." Trying to play it off, she took another bite of her pizza, then said, "It's important to be in the know."

"Samantha." I waited until her eyes met mine and then said, "As long as you are with me, I'll do everything in my power to make you happy. You want to take that job in Nashville, then take it. We'll find a way to make it work until you can get something here. You want a house? I'll buy you a house— the biggest, nicest house you've ever seen. You want some fancy apartment by the river? I'll make it happen. You want kids? I'll give you as many as you want and love and protect them until the day I take my last breath."

Tears filled her eyes as she muttered, "Gus."

"I mean it, Sam. I take care of the people who are important to me, and you're on the top of that list. I'm just asking for a little time. Can you give me that?"

"Yes." She nodded as she leaned towards me and wrapped her arms around my neck, hugging me tightly. "I can give you that."

"Good. Now, finish your pizza, 'cause as soon as this movie is over, I'm gonna be wanting another go." I kissed her on the cheek as I said, "I still can't get that fucking dress out of my head."

She eased back on the bed and smiled. "I think I'm gonna have to get me a few more of those little, black dresses."

"If you do, you better be ready to suffer the consequences."

"I'm more than ready."

When we finished eating, Samantha curled up next to me, and we turned our attention back to the movie we'd been watching. As soon as it was over, we made love again, and by the time I was done with her, she was completely spent and had fallen asleep in my arms.

After the club's encounter with the Ravens, we all struggled to come to terms with the loss of one of our brothers and a prospect—especially me. It was my job to keep my boys out of harm's way, and it gutted me that I'd failed them. Samantha knew something wasn't right, but she didn't push. While she was still learning the ins and outs of the club life, she understood that there were things I simply couldn't, and wouldn't, share with her.

Things were just starting to get settled down with the club when Sam mentioned a possible job transfer to Nashville. I'd barely had a chance to wrap my head around the news when her mother had shown up for an unexpected visit. I knew from the moment we'd met that she wasn't happy about us being together. It wasn't like she tried to hide the fact, and even though Samantha tried to deny it, I knew it got to her. I wasn't blind. I could see the worry in her eyes, the wheels turning in her head whenever she was at the clubhouse. Even though Samantha and I were from two different worlds, traveling on two completely different paths, I could also feel the love she felt for me whenever she was in my arms.

But as I lay there watching her sleep, a thought crossed my mind, causing a knot to twist in my gut. I was a man who had it all. I had my club, my brothers—my family, and I had a woman who I loved like no other. This realization should've made me fucking ecstatic, but I knew how things worked. No man could have it all forever, and the same would hold true for me. I didn't know how and I didn't when, but the tides of change were coming.

GUS

TWENTY-FIVE YEARS LATER

I was right about the tides of change. They came with a vengeance, ripping my heart right out of my fucking chest. They carried it so far out to sea, I never thought I'd get it back. Didn't figure I needed it anyway. Samantha—the only woman I ever truly cared about—walked out on me. Damn. I'd loved that woman like no other. Would've moved heaven and earth for her, and all I'd gotten in return was a note left next to my pillow. Even after she'd given me the shaft, I was foolish enough to think she might come back to me. Hell, I waited over a year for Samantha to find her way back to me, but that never happened. I didn't get so much as a fucking phone call, so I bit the bullet and went to find her on my own. That's when I discovered that she'd married another—a man who fit into her life in a way that I never could.

It was a hard hit. I didn't want to accept the fact that I'd lost her, but I didn't have a choice. I did the only thing I could. I put Samantha behind me and committed my full focus to my brothers and the club. I continued to build our numbers with men who I could trust and knew would always remain loyal to the brotherhood. In doing so, I managed to build one of the most powerful MCs in the South. While there were those who'd tried to take us down, we still remained on top, and there wasn't a soul around who didn't know the Satan's Fury name and what we represented. Memphis was our territory, and if I had anything to say about it, that would never change.

Even though I took a great deal of pride in what I had accomplished, I'd always felt like there was something missing in my life. I knew that it was Samantha I was longing for. It hadn't been easy letting her go. Hell, I'm not sure I ever really did. I'd spent twenty-five years wondering what had gone wrong, but never came up with any real answers. I didn't want to accept the fact that I'd never see her again, but I wasn't really given a fucking choice. Then, one day, a young woman came walking into the clubhouse, and I felt like my whole world had been turned upside down—again.

She was a pretty, little thing. Young with long, dark hair and dark eyes like my own. I'd never met the girl, but there was something oddly familiar about her. Her voice trembled as she asked, "Are you Gus?"

"I am." I studied her for a moment, trying to figure out how I might know her, but I just couldn't put my finger on it. "What can I do for you?"

"I'm August ... *August James*." The name didn't trigger any memory, making me even more curious as to why she'd come to the clubhouse looking for me. "My mother sent me here from Nashville. She said if anyone could help me, it would be you."

"And why would she say that?"

"I have no idea. I was hoping you could answer that."

"All right, well … let's start with her." She wasn't giving me much to go on, so I crossed my arms and asked, "Who's your mother?"

"Samantha Rayburn."

In my gut, I knew exactly who she was talking about, but I had to be sure. "Samantha Rayburn?"

"I think you knew her by her maiden name. *Samantha Travers*. She married my father, Denis Rayburn."

And there it was. The answer I knew was coming. I couldn't believe that after all these years, I'd actually hear *that* name again. I suddenly felt like I'd been hit by a Mack truck, and all those feelings—the anger, the heartache and bitterness—I'd forced myself to suppress, instantly came creeping back. August stood there waiting for some kind of response, but I was rendered speechless. All my words were caught in my throat, and there was nothing I could do but stand there and stare at her. After several moments, she finally asked, "Do you remember her?"

"Yeah, I remember her," I answered with an angry tone. I knew it wasn't fair to her. She wasn't the one who'd fucked me over, but I just couldn't seem to get a grip on myself.

"I'm sorry to come unannounced like this, but I had no other way of reaching you." Clearly nervous, she shifted her stance as she clenched her fists at her sides. "Mom tried to find it, but she didn't have your number."

"Yeah. I'm guessing she lost it a long time ago." As I stood there looking at her, an unbelievable thought crossed my mind. I'm not even sure what made me consider it, but I found myself asking, "I'm just curious. How old are you?"

"I'm twenty-four."

"Hmm." I could feel my temperature rising as the pieces started to fit together. Even though I already knew the answer, I asked, "When were you born?"

"April of '95." Her eyes narrowed as she asked, "Why?"

A little basic math, and it all became crystal clear. Fuck me. It was hard to even look at her. I thought I'd felt betrayed when Samantha had left with no real explanation, but finding out that I had a daughter I never knew about was a betrayal like none other. "She wouldn't … Damn it!"

Surprised by my reaction, August asked, "Am I missing something here? Did I say something wrong?"

If it wasn't actually happening right there in front of me, I wouldn't have believed it, but it was clear from her expression that she was clueless as to why I was so upset. "You don't know?"

"I have no idea what you're talking about, so apparently not."

"Of course, she didn't." Not only had she kept the truth from me, she'd kept the truth from our daughter. "Damn it all to hell."

I needed a minute to collect myself before I did or said something I regretted, so I stormed out of the bar and into the parking lot. I inhaled a deep breath and tried to calm myself down, but I was too fucking angry. I felt like I was about to explode. I wanted to break something. I wanted to wrap my fingers around someone's neck and choke them, make them suffer the pain I was feeling at that moment. It was all too much. My daughter was grown. I wasn't there the day she was born. I didn't get to see her take her first steps, lose her first tooth, or even go out on her first fucking date. I'd missed it—all of it. I wanted to know why. I wanted to know what I'd done to deserve this kind of betrayal. There was only one person who could answer those questions, and she wasn't there to answer them.

Having no other choice, I swallowed back my anger, my pride, and I went back into the bar. I walked straight over to August and said, "I need you to tell me. Why did Samantha send you here?"

"I'm really sorry if I said something to upset you. I didn't mean to say the wrong thing or ..."

"No. It's not anything you did, August." I hated that I'd upset her. None of this was her fault, but that didn't change the fact that I wanted to know what was going on. "Now, I need you to answer the question."

"Because there is no one else who can help me." Tears filled her eyes as she continued, "My daughter, Harper, is missing. She disappeared three days ago."

I'd never been a man who liked surprises. I surrounded myself with people who made sure I always knew what was coming. But this? Hell no. I didn't have a clue about any of it. I had no idea that I had a daughter, much less a granddaughter, and discovering that Samantha sent August to me to help find her daughter, Harper—my granddaughter—was like adding salt to the wound. I couldn't understand why she would've kept August away from me for all those years only to send her to me when trouble had come knocking at her door. I couldn't understand why I never got the chance to be there for the good fucking times, too, but that was a question that would have to wait for another day. My granddaughter was in danger, and now that I actually knew that she even existed, I would be damned if I was going to let anything happen to her.

August went on to tell me all the details about how Harper had been taken from her daycare three days ago. The police hadn't been able to locate her, and she was becoming desperate. "Have you or your husband gotten any notes or phone calls about a ransom?"

"*Ex-husband*, and no. At least, I haven't. I have no idea about David." A look of disgust crossed her face as she said, "My ex-husband has been putting on a good front, talking to the media and pretending to be distraught over his daughter's disappearance, but honestly, I think it's just for show."

"What makes you say that?"

"Because I know David. He'd just as soon tell a lie than the truth, and he's pretty damn good at it too. That's why he's always made such a great politician."

"Wait. *David James*, as in David James the mayor of Nashville? That's your ex-husband?"

"That would be him."

"Damn." Other than what I'd seen on TV, I didn't know much about the guy. From what I could tell, he seemed to be in his mid-forties, so I asked, "He's a good bit older than you, right?"

"Yes. Seventeen years older to be exact."

There was something in her tone that made me think she was more than just a little suspicious of him, so I asked, "You think he's the one who took her?"

"No, but I think he might know who did."

We talked a little longer, and she told me everything I'd need to know to find Harper. Even though the timing wasn't great with our big run coming up, I assured her that I would do what I could to find Harper. I asked Gunner to take her down to one of the rooms, but before he did, I had to ask, "Your mother? She live in Nashville too?"

"Yeah. She's still in the same house where I grew up. It's about twenty minutes from me."

"Has she been doing okay?"

"I guess. For the most part anyway ... she's worried sick about Harper, but she's holding it together."

I was still pretty fucked up about finding out that she'd kept August from me, but I hadn't heard anything from her in years. Since she never came back, I could only assume that she'd felt she'd made the right decision when she left. Curious to know if it had all been worth it, I asked, "Is she happy?"

"When I was a kid, I thought she was happy, but now, looking back, I'm not so sure. She's had to face some hard times, more than her fair share, but she always tried to focus on the positive side of things and encouraged me to do the same."

"Yeah, I remember that about her." I turned to leave, but stopped and asked, "Hey ... You ever wonder where you got the name August?"

"It's not exactly a common name, is it?" she scoffed with a shrug. "I just figured Mom was trying to come up with something unique. I figured it was the month she got pregnant with me or something like that?"

"Yeah, I guess that could be a possibility."

With that, Gunner took her down to one of the empty rooms while I went to my office and made a few calls. I had some connections in Nashville and hoped they might be able to help me find some answers. I started with

Viper, the president of the Ruthless Sinners. I told him what was going on, and he assured me that he'd find out whatever he could about David James. After I made a few more calls, I asked Murphy, Riggs, and Gunner to come down to my office. Once they'd all come in and sat down, I told them, "I've got something to discuss with you boys, but I'm trusting you to keep this conversation between us. What's said in this room, stays in this room. Is that understood?"

"Understood," they each replied.

"I wouldn't even be telling you any of this, but you need to know how important this all is to me."

I spent the next half-hour telling them about my relationship with Samantha and how I suspected that August was my daughter. "If August is mine, then that means it's my granddaughter who's out there missing. We have to find her."

"I'm here to help you any way I can," Murphy assured me. "We all are."

"I appreciate that, brother." I wasn't surprised by their response. My boys had never failed to have my back. I turned to Gunner and told him, "I want you keeping an eye on August. I'm trusting you to make sure nothing happens to her."

"You can count on me, Prez."

"Always have." I ran my hand over my beard as I told them, "I put a call into the Ruthless Sinners' clubhouse and spoke to their prez, Viper. He's putting feelers out to see if he can come up with anything on Harper. While I was at it, I asked him about the mayor."

"And?" Riggs pushed.

"He said he's all kinds of shady. Far from the up and

up, so August might be right about him knowing more about Harper than he's letting on."

"Damn, that makes things complicated."

"Yeah, but it doesn't matter. In case there's any question, I'm gonna find her, and when I do, she better be okay or I'm gonna fucking end whoever took her."

After doing a little digging, the boys and I discovered that August's piece-of-shit ex-husband, David, was a crooked politician. Hoping to win his election, he'd gotten into bed with Anthony Polito, an Italian mafia boss with a rap sheet a mile long. We had a talk with August, found out where we could find David, and I sent Shadow and Riggs to go get him. They brought him back to the clubhouse, and we took him straight to one of Shadow's rooms. He was our club's enforcer, and he had a knack for making men spill their secrets. David was no different. After a few hard blows, he started singing like a fucking canary. He admitted that he had a connection to Polito, that he'd taken bribes to win his election, but it took another round with Shadow hammering into him to get him to confess everything.

"Polito. He's the one who took her. He th-thought I'd make good on my promise if he held my daughter's life over my head. He didn't get the fact that I can't just snap my fingers and get his guy off. It took some time, but I got … it sorted. I've got it worked out where his guy will be able to get out on bail. Once that happens, Polito will return Harper and this thing will be over."

"And what happens if this guy is considered some kind of flight risk and doesn't get bail?"

"He'll get bail," he answered adamantly. "I pulled a few strings and got him on Judge Michaels' docket. He owes me a favor, and we also have a witness that will testify that the cops didn't give him his Miranda rights. That by itself is enough to get the charges dropped."

"How will he get Harper back to you?"

"As soon as the hearing is over, we'll meet up with him somewhere. Probably at the diner where we've met before. It's not a big deal. I swear it."

I couldn't believe my ears. This asshole didn't seemed bothered in the least that his own child had been kidnapped. "It's your daughter, asshole. It's a big fucking deal!"

"That's not what I meant. I know it's a big deal, and I'm telling you ... I'll get her back."

"You better hope the hell you do, because if you don't ... if so much as one hair is touched on her pretty little head, I'll end you with my bare hands." I took a charging step towards him as I growled, "I have a half a mind to go on and do it right now after the hell you've put August through."

"August? Is she h-how I ended up here?"

"She came to us out of concern for her daughter," I snapped. "If you were any kind of man at all, you'd get that."

"I should've known she had something to do with this. *Dammit!* She couldn't just leave it alone," he complained. "That fucking ... cunt has been a pain in my ass for two and a half years now. Always on my ass. Bitching and moaning when I can't make it to Harper's goddamn birthday party. *Fuck.* It's not like she won't have another one. I should've saved m-myself the hassle and had her dealt with ages ago."

Consumed with rage, I reared back and slammed my

fist into his jaw. Before he had a chance to recover, I hit him again and again, knocking him completely out. When his head dropped, I muttered, "Worthless piece of shit."

I wanted to do more. Hell, I wanted to kill the motherfucker, but I knew that wasn't an option. Instead, I left him hanging in that room until the following morning when it was time to go pick up Harper from Polito. When the time came for us to leave for Nashville, Shadow and I took David with us in our SUV, while Gunner and Riggs took August in theirs. David had made arrangements to meet up with Polito at a restaurant downtown. He seemed confident that the drop-off would go without a hitch. Thankfully, he was right. I dropped him off at the rear parking lot, and it wasn't long before he was walking back with Harper in his arms.

I have to admit getting Harper back was bittersweet. While I was relieved that she was safe and sound, I hadn't gotten much time to spend with August and only a few fleeting moments with my granddaughter. Gunner, Riggs, Shadow and I were in the parking lot with August, watching as David returned Harper. After exchanging a few words, David stormed off. Once he was gone, I went over to say my goodbyes. When I walked over to August and Harper, Shadow asked, "Is it just me, or was that too fucking easy? Polito just handed her over ... no questions asked. Doesn't seem right."

"That's because it isn't." I hated to think of those men coming after Harper or August, but like it or not, it was a real possibility. "If they took her, there's nothing to keep them from doing it again, or worse. We're going to have to find a way to make sure that shit doesn't happen."

August clutched her daughter close to her chest as she asked, "How are you going to do that?"

"Let us worry about that. You just focus on having your daughter back." I looked over at my beautiful daughter and granddaughter, and I suddenly found it hard to breathe. They were mine—both of them. I so desperately wanted to tell them the truth, to tell everyone, but the time just wasn't right. I placed my hand on Harper's little head as I said, "Her pictures didn't do her justice. She's beautiful like her momma."

"Thank you, Gus." August leaned towards me, hugging me tightly.

"No need to thank me, August. It was my pleasure." I gave her a quick squeeze in return, then took a step back and turned to Gunner. He'd been watching over August while she was at the clubhouse. I figured she'd feel the safest with him around, so I told him, "I'm gonna need you to hang back and stay with them for a couple of days to keep an eye on things."

There was no missing the concern in her voice when she asked, "Do you really think that's necessary?"

"Don't want to take any chances." I hadn't checked with him first, so I looked back at Gunner and asked, "You good with staying? Need anything?"

"I'm good. Got a change of clothes in the truck."

My mind was racing as I followed them back over to the SUV. I didn't want her to go. I wanted her to come back to Memphis, so I could get to know the daughter I never knew I had. I wanted to talk to her, tell her the things that were going through my head, but I needed to wait until the time was right. For now, I had to let her go. Just before she got inside, I called out to her, "August?"

"Yeah?"

"I got something I need to discuss with you." I tried to hide the uneasiness I was feeling, but I'm pretty sure she saw right through me. "Now isn't the time, but I would like to get in touch with you soon. You okay with that?"

"Yeah. Absolutely. I'm definitely okay with that." She studied me for a minute then asked, "Is something wrong?"

"Nothing for you to worry about. Just some unfinished business." I glanced down at Harper, ran my hand over her head as I tried to commit her face to my memory. After several moments, I looked back to August. Damn. She was everything I could've hoped for in a daughter. I just hated I'd missed so much of her life. As I stood there staring at her, I made a vow to myself to make up for the time I'd lost. "I'll be in touch soon."

"Okay." She smiled, then said, "I'll be looking forward to it."

I helped her get Harper inside the SUV, and once they were settled, I closed the door and watched as they drove out of the parking lot. As much as I hated to see them go, I found comfort in knowing that I would be seeing them again, and if I had anything to say about it, it would be sooner than later.

SAMANTHA

*S*ending August to see Gus was harder than I could've imagined. I wouldn't have even suggested it if I'd thought there was another way for us to get Harper back, but we were desperate. August was completely distraught and was barely holding it together. I wasn't much better. Harper meant the world to us both. After August divorced David, they spent a great deal of time with me, and I'd gotten very attached to Harper. For such a small child, she brought so much light into my life, and when we discovered that she was missing, it was like our whole world had been turned upside down. We searched everywhere for her, even places the police didn't think to look. August hired a private investigator, but he was no help either. I felt so helpless. No one had been able to give us any answers, and time was getting away from us. We had to do something, so I decided it was time for August to go see Gus. If anyone could find Harper, I knew it would be him.

I could still remember the look on August's face when

I told her she should go see him. We'd both had a long night. She'd come home after talking with David, and she was crying hysterically as she told me about their conversation. She was adamant that he knew who had taken Harper, but she had no way of proving it. We both felt like we should be doing something more, so we got in the car and just started driving around, hoping by chance we might spot Harper somewhere. When we could barely keep our eyes open a minute longer, we drove back to the house and went to bed. I couldn't sleep. I kept thinking about Gus. I'd gone back and forth with whether or not I should mention him to her, but eventually decided he was our only hope.

The sun was just starting to rise as we made ourselves a cup of coffee and sat down at the kitchen table. Tears started to fill her eyes once again as she looked over to me and said, "I've got to do something. I can't keep going on like this."

"I know, sweetheart. I've been thinking the same thing. I think I know someone who might be able to help."

Confusion crossed her face as she looked up at me and asked, "Who?"

"It's nobody that you know. He's just an old friend of mine." I suddenly felt anxious, like I was walking on a slippery slope as I continued, "His name is Gus, and he's in Memphis."

"How's a guy in Memphis going to be able to help me find Harper?"

"I don't know how to explain it." I let out a deep breath. "You're just going to have to trust me on this."

"Who is this guy?"

"He's a friend, but he knows people, August. The kind of people who can help us get Harper back."

Her eyes narrowed as she asked, "Is this guy dangerous or something?"

"He can help, sweetheart. That's all you need to know."

"So, you say he's a friend or whatever, but how do you know that he'll even help me find Harper?" she pushed.

"Because he will." I placed my hand on hers as I said, "You just have to go see him face to face. Tell him that I sent you and that Harper is missing. Once you do that, he'll do whatever it takes to find her."

As she wiped the tears from her cheek, she said, "You sound pretty sure of yourself."

"That's because I am." I could've told her the truth about Gus then, but I just didn't know how—not after all this time. "You need to go see him today. Now, actually."

"Why me? Why don't you call him or go talk to him for me?"

"Because you are Harper's mother. It will be better coming from you."

"I don't know, Mom." Her brows furrowed. "It seems kind of strange to go see some guy I don't even know and ask him for help."

"Do you want to find Harper?"

"You know that I do."

"Then get in your car and go see him," I demanded. "The sooner you get to him, the sooner we'll get Harper back."

August stood as she asked, "Are you sure about this?"

"I've never been more sure about anything."

"Okay. I guess it's worth a try." She got up and started for the door, then stopped. "Wait. What am I doing? I have no idea how to find this guy."

"You'll go downtown, by the river... It's a large, cobblestone building with a tall gated fence around it."

"Mom, you're not giving me much to go by here."

"I know. I'm sorry." I couldn't remember the exact address, so I told her, "Go to the Peabody. Take Third down to McLemore. When you get there, if you don't see it, stop and ask someone for directions."

"Directions to a guy name Gus?"

"Tell them you're looking for the Satan's Fury clubhouse."

"Clubhouse?"

I wasn't surprised by her question. I knew she had no idea what I was talking about. She didn't know anything about MCs or bikers in general. Hell, she wouldn't know a Fury man even if he walked right up to her, but there weren't many around Memphis who hadn't heard of Gus and his brothers. I had no doubt that someone would be able to help her find it. "They'll tell you exactly where to go."

Thankfully, she didn't push for more information. Instead, she went to change her clothes, then quickly returned to the kitchen. With a look of determination, she took her keys and her purse in her hand and rushed out the door. I followed her outside and waited as she got in her car. Before she took off, she rolled down her window and said, "Stay by your phone. I'll call you when I get there."

"Okay. Will do."

I watched as she pulled out of the driveway, and once she was no longer in sight, I went back inside. My nerves were shot and I felt like I couldn't breathe, so I went straight into the kitchen and took out a bottle of bourbon from the cabinet. I quickly poured some into my glass, then drank it. Without even giving it a chance to take the edge off, I poured myself another one, then carried it into the living room and sat down. I took in several long, cleansing breaths, trying my best not to completely unravel, but I couldn't help myself. I'd just sent August to meet her father for the first time. They were flesh and blood, and yet, they were both complete strangers. Finding out that I'd kept the truth from them for all these years would be hard on them both. They would be angry with me, probably hate me, but it was a chance I had to take. Gus was our only hope of finding Harper, and honestly, I was relieved that the truth would soon be out.

I sat there watching the clock, and as each hour passed, I became more and more anxious. I remembered the first time I'd gone to the Satan's Fury clubhouse. It was a day I would never forget, and I had a feeling my daughter would feel the same way. Like me, she'd never really been around bikers. Their way of life was quite different from ours. They were rougher, tougher, and it might take her some time to see that behind their hard exteriors they were good men, especially Gus. I've never known a man who was so caring, so compassionate, and loyal to his family. There was nothing he wouldn't do for his brothers, and I hoped the same would hold true for August.

Other than a quick call to check directions, I hadn't heard anything from August in hours. I just sat there in that living room, lost in my own head, waiting to hear something. I was considering making myself another drink when my phone rang. As I'd hoped, it was August letting me know that she'd found her way to the clubhouse.

"Did you talk to Gus? Is he going to help you find Harper?"

"He's going to try."

"Oh, thank god." I couldn't have been more relieved. I knew in my heart that if anyone could find her, it would be him. "Did you tell him about the daycare and—"

"I told him everything, Mom."

"Good. Then, he'll find her."

"You really think so? Cause I'm not going to be able to survive if something happens to Harper."

"We're going to find her, sweetheart, and I really do think

Gus will help us get some answers," I assured her. "That's more than anyone has been able to do."

"I hope you're right."

"I am. You'll see."

She paused for a moment, and then asked a question I'd hoped she wouldn't ask. "What's the deal with you and this Gus guy?"

"I've already told you. He's an old friend of mine."

"I know that's what you told me, Mom, but I've got a feeling there's a lot you aren't telling me about him ... and his club." Her tone was borderline sarcastic as she said, "I wouldn't think that these are the kind of people you would've run around with, at least not with Gran around."

"I met Gus when I was still living in Memphis. He helped me when some guy tried to steal my purse." Just thinking back to that night brought a smile to my face. He was so damn handsome and charming—something I wouldn't have expected from a tough as nails biker, but he was, just the same. Falling for him was easy, but it made leaving him even that much harder. I didn't want to get into all that, so I simply told her, "We spent some time together, but that ended when I accepted a job in Nashville. I started seeing your father shortly after, so I lost ties with Gus. Simple as that."

"So, you guys dated?"

"Yes." I felt like I was opening a door that didn't need to be opened, so I tried to keep things as simple as I could. "It's hard to explain, sweetheart. Just remember ... you can't always judge a book by its cover."

"Maybe not, but some things are hard to overlook."

"It's not as hard as you might think." I knew I shouldn't, but I couldn't stop myself from asking, "By the way, how is he?"

"Gus?" She paused for a moment, then answered, "Umm,

fine. I guess. He kind of freaked out when I told him I was your daughter."

I could only imagine how he felt when he found out that she was my daughter. Knowing Gus, I felt fairly certain that he'd been able to put two and two together and realized that August was his daughter. "Did he seem angry?"

"It's hard to say what he was feeling. He stormed out of the clubhouse for a few minutes, but when he came back, he seemed okay. That's when I told him all about Harper. After I finished telling him everything, he asked about you."

"He did?"

"Yeah. He wanted to know how you were doing and if you were happy."

"Oh." Considering how I'd left things, I wouldn't have thought he'd even care how I was, much less if I was happy. "That kind of surprises me."

"Why wouldn't he, especially if you two dated?"

"It's complicated." It was time for me to change the subject, so I asked her, "Have you heard anything from David or the police?"

"I got a call from Detective Haralson earlier, but I wasn't able to take it. I should call him back."

"Okay. Keep me posted."

"You know I will."

I spent the next couple of days waiting on pins and needles to hear whether or not Gus had been able to get Harper back. Thankfully, things worked out exactly as they'd all hoped, and August called to tell me that Harper was back from the men who took her and she was safe and sound. I couldn't have been more relieved. I knew fate was working her hand, and it wouldn't be long until I had to answer for all the secrets I'd kept.

GUS

*T*he days after Harper's return were pretty much a blur. We'd just completed another big run, and I had a shit ton of work to catch up on. I was grateful for the distraction, but every time I got a second to catch my breath, my mind would drift back to August and Samantha. I just couldn't figure out how things had gotten so fucked up. Samantha and I had a good thing once, a real good thing, and it was hard to believe that she would just walk away without some kind of reason. There was always the chance that I could've been wrong about everything. Maybe she didn't feel like the club life was for her or maybe she simply didn't love me the way I thought she did. That thought got to me the most. I figured in time I'd get the answers I was looking for—one way or another. I knew that. I just had no idea that they'd be coming sooner than later.

I was in the garage going over inventory with Blaze when my burner started to ring. When I saw that it was Gunner, I figured he was just gonna tell me that he was on his way back. I was wrong. There was no hiding the concern in his voice as he told me, "Pres, we've got trouble."

Having no idea what he was talking about, I asked, "What kind of trouble?"

"Three black BMWs just pulled up at August's place, and Gus, these guys didn't look like they were fucking around. They were packing, and there were too fucking many of them for me to take out on my own."

While I knew there was a chance Polito would be back, I'd hoped we'd seen the end of him. Just thinking of August and Harper being in danger made my blood boil. "Fuck! Where are you now?"

"We swiped a van, and we're heading into downtown."

"Are Harper and August with you?"

"Yes, and Samantha, too."

A cold chill ran down my spine at the sound of Samantha's name. I tried to hide my reaction. "Good. You did the right thing getting the hell out of there. Get them over to the Sinners' clubhouse. I'll text you the address." I was doing my best to keep a level head. "The boys and I'll be there as soon as we can."

"Will do."

After I hung up the phone, I gathered up several of the guys and explained the situation with August. It was no surprise that they all agreed to help me deal with Polito. Even though he wanted to join us, I asked Moose, my VP, to stay behind and keep an on things at the club. As soon as we were packed, the guys and I were on our way to Nashville. It was just a three-hour drive, even less with my driving a hundred miles an hour, but I couldn't get there fast enough. Hell, I needed to get a fucking grip, but

I couldn't stop thinking about what might've happened if Gunner hadn't been there with August and Harper. It was irrational thinking, but the fear of losing them was crippling. To make matters worse, I was trying to wrap my head around the fact that I was about to see Samantha for the first time in twenty-five years. I thought I'd have more time to prepare myself to see the woman I'd loved for an eternity—the woman who'd left and taken my child along with her. I'd like to say that the drive had given me time to collect myself, but it didn't. I was just as fucked up as ever when we finally got to the Sinners' clubhouse in Nashville.

I was done fucking around. I wanted Polito dead. Hell, I wanted David dead, too, but he was the fucking mayor of Nashville. We couldn't exactly end him without backlash, so we'd come up with another plan for him. Our immediate threat was Polito, and we set our focus on him. With Riggs's help, we were able to locate all the properties Polito owned in the area. Riggs and Hammer, the Sinners' computer hacker, would do what they could to break into their security systems. We needed to be able to see exactly how many men he had on his payroll, all the entry and exit points, and what kind of artillery they were carrying. It had barely been two days since we'd arrived, but a plan was starting to unfolded—one that would end Polito for good.

After a long day of hashing out plans, we all gathered at the bar for a drink. I was sitting at the bar with T-Bone and the others when I spotted August talking to Hawk. I didn't think much about it until I noticed the look on Gunner's face. It was an expression I'd seen many times, but I wasn't expecting to see it from him—at least not directed towards my daughter. "Fuck me. I've seen that look before."

"Huh?" The blood drained from his face when he realized his secret was out. "Prez, I've been meaning to talk you about her, but—"

I was his president, and he knew there was a good chance that August was my daughter. Getting involved with her would mean putting everything on the line and he knew it. "Knowing what you know, you gotta have balls to go there."

"Not like that … You gotta know, I didn't mean for it to happen," he tried to explain. "Hell, I tried to fight it the best I could, but she got to me. Got under my skin like no woman ever has. The kid, too."

"I trusted you."

"I know you did, and I wouldn't do anything to fuck that up." I could hear the sincerity in his voice, but that didn't matter. I was his president. I'd been good to him. The brothers had been good to him, and he was willing to turn his back on all that in order to claim my daughter as his ol' lady. "I care about her, Gus. More than I even realized."

"Fuck, Gunner. I got too fucking much to deal with right now. I don't need this shit, too."

"I get that. I wish I could tell you that I would walk away if that's what you wanted, but I just can't do that."

He glanced back over at August, and by the way he was looking at her, there was no doubt he truly cared for her. While I wasn't thrilled about the idea, Gunner was a good man. From the day he started prospecting, his loyalty to me and the brothers never wavered. Hell, he'd taken more than a couple of bullets for us, and I'm sure he'd take a few more. Remembering how her mother got to me, I turned to him and said, "She'll end up breaking your heart. The good ones always do."

"I'm willing to take that chance, besides … the damage is already done. I want her, brother. Nothing I won't do to have her."

"Suit yourself, but you fuck this up—you hurt her or Harper, and you'll have to deal with me."

He knew exactly what I meant. If he caused any harm to come to either of them, I'd make him regret it in ways he'd never dreamed fathomable. Gunner nodded as he answered, "Understood."

"I've always thought a lot of you. You're like a son to me, Gunner. Don't fuck that up."

"I won't. You have my word."

"Good." I motioned my hand over towards August and Hawk, then said, "Now, it looks like you have some business to tend to. Wouldn't want Hawk thinking she was free for the taking."

"Yeah, I have every intention of setting him straight."

Just about that time, I noticed Samantha was heading towards the exit. Before she walked out of the room, she glanced back in my direction, and my chest tightened the second our eyes met. Damn. Even after all these years, she could still get to me with a single look. As soon as she walked out of the room, I stood up and turned to the others as I said, "I've got some business to tend to."

I left the bar and headed straight to the room where Samantha had been staying. When I reached her door, my anger was at a boiling point, and yet my longing to just be in the same room with her again was overwhelming. The two emotions were fighting each other, and as I knocked on her door, I had no idea which one would win. I inhaled a deep breath, trying to collect myself as I waited for her to answer. When the door finally opened, I quickly realized I was in more trouble than I thought. She was wearing nothing but a short, white t-shirt, and she looked fucking incredible. My eyes dropped to her long, lean legs, and I could remember how good they felt wrapped around me. Pulling me from that memory, she whispered, "Did you need something?"

"Yeah." Without waiting to be invited, I stepped inside her room. "We need to talk."

"Okay." She closed the door, then turned to me with an anxious expression. "What exactly do you want to talk about?"

"There are so many things, I don't even know where to start," I grumbled under my breath. Once I made my way across the room, I leaned against the edge of the desk with my arms crossed and silently studied her for a moment. When Samantha was younger, she was a beautiful woman with gorgeous, long blonde hair, and eyes that seemed to see right through to your soul. She had a smile that could melt the coldest of hearts, even mine, and even after all these years, she was still just as beautiful as she was all those years ago—if not more. As she stood there staring back at me, I remembered how soft her skin used to feel beneath my fingertips, and it was impossible not to wonder if she still felt the same. Then, it hit me. I'd know the answer if she hadn't walked out on me. Sounding angrier than I'd intended, I growled, "Why didn't you just tell me that I wasn't who you wanted?"

"I did want you, Gus. I wanted you more than anything in this world." My gut twisted into a knot when

Samantha looked at me with longing in her eyes. I tried to fight it, but I suddenly felt that familiar pull I'd always had towards her. I shouldn't have been surprised. I'd wanted her back in my life for so damn long, and she was right there, standing in front of me looking just as gorgeous as she always had. It was fucking with my head. Her eyes filled with tears as she stepped towards me. "You just don't understand. You'll never know how hard it was for me to walk away."

"Then why don't you explain it to me, because that note you left next to my pillow twenty-five years ago didn't tell me a damn thing!" I could still remember how she looked at me, the hunger that burned in her eyes every time we were close; the way she said my name, there was no denying the sound of love in her voice, and the way she kissed me, damn, it was like she couldn't get enough of me. I felt the same damn way about her. I just couldn't understand how she could just walk away from that. "I went to bed thinking we had a good thing. Woke up to you gone, and I never even knew why. You got any idea what that does to a man, Samantha? When you rip his heart out and don't even tell him why?"

It was torture listening to the anguish in her voice as she responded, "I didn't have a choice, Gus. I knew if I stayed and told you what was going on, you would've tried to convince me not to leave. You would've tried to work it out, but there was no way that could've happened. My mother would've ruined you, and you would've ended up hating me. I couldn't let that happen."

"Your mother?" I thought back to the night when I'd met her mother for the first time—so prim and proper. She greeted me with a smile, but I could see the repulsion in her eyes when she looked at me. It was clear she wasn't happy that I was seeing her daughter, but I figured in time, she'd learn to get over it. "What the hell does she have to do with you leaving?"

"It's a long story."

"Under the circumstances, I think I deserve to hear it, don't you?"

"Fine. I'll tell you, but you aren't going to like what I have to say." She paused for a moment, then started, "You might remember that my father was campaigning for governor when we were seeing each other. He'd made a lot of sacrifices to get to that point in his career. We all had." She turned with her back facing me as she lowered her head and thought for a moment. "The media was watching his every move, and not just his. They were watching us all, so when my mother found out that we were together, she was furious with me. She thought it would hurt my father's reputation if his daughter was seeing a biker." She turned around, and as her eyes met mine, I knew she was telling me the truth when she said, "I tried to explain to her that you were a good man and I loved you, but she wouldn't listen. I know it sounds ridiculous, but she was adamant that I end things and was furious when I refused."

"You never told me that she felt that way."

"I didn't think it mattered. I loved you and wanted to be with you. I didn't care what she thought or what the media thought." She wrapped her arms around herself as she inhaled a deep breath. "I thought, in time, she would learn to accept our relationship, but that didn't happen. Instead, she found a way to make sure we could never be together."

"What the hell are you talking about?"

"She had someone watching you." Before I'd had a chance to truly register what she'd said, she continued, "It was a long time ago. I'm not sure if you remember, but you were having some troubles with the club. You wouldn't tell me what those problems were, but I knew they were bad. I just didn't know how bad."

"You're gonna have to give me more than that, Samantha."

"The guy … he had a video of you and the guys at some warehouse. I have to admit, I was surprised by what I saw on that video. You never shared that part of your life with me." She inhaled a deep breath and let it out slowly. "It was hard to see everything, but there was a lot of gunfire. It showed you shooting a man. And not only you. Moose, T-Bone, and a few of the others were all involved in the shooting. Together, you killed six men, but you didn't stop there. You also burned down the warehouse to cover your tracks. It's all on that video. Mom threatened to take that video to the police if I didn't stop seeing you."

I remembered that night all too well, and hearing that someone had recorded me and my brothers made me feel like someone had just pulled the rug from beneath my feet. I couldn't believe it. I'd fucked up. I'd fucked up big. I wasn't a man who made mistakes like that, not even back then. I always watched my back. I couldn't believe I'd actually had someone tailing me and didn't even fucking know it. A mistake like that could've cost me more than just the woman I loved. It could've cost me everything. In barely a whisper, I grumbled, "*Fuck.*"

"I knew if I told you about it, you'd say you didn't care … that we'd find a way to work it out. But I knew my mother, Gus. She'd made up her mind that she didn't want us together, and with her and my father's connections, she would've made it impossible for us to keep seeing one another." I couldn't believe what I was hearing. My worst nightmare had become a reality, and I didn't even know it. The thought made me angry. So very angry. Angry with Samantha. Her mother. Angry with myself. I should've been more careful, and then I wouldn't have lost her. I wouldn't have put my boys in danger. "You would've ended up in jail. You and your brothers. You would've lost everything that you worked so hard to build, and they would've blamed you for it. They would've known that your connection to me cost them their freedom and everything they cared about. I couldn't let that happen. I loved you too much."

"You should've told me."

"What difference would it have made? The end result would've been the same," she argued. "At least, this way you were able to have your life. Your club. Your brothers."

A part of me knew she was right, but I wanted to believe that I could've fixed things if I'd had the chance— if she'd just trusted me enough to talk to me. "But I didn't have you, and I didn't have my daughter!"

"You know about August?"

"Her birthday. *Her name*. Yeah, it didn't take much to connect the dots. The fucked-up part of all this? I would have never known I even had a daughter if Harper hadn't been in danger."

"I think that's one of the reasons I sent her to you … I was hoping that you would find out. That the truth would finally come out."

"That's one hell of a way for the truth to come out. Not

only do I find out that I have daughter, but also a grand-daughter, and that she was missing. You got any idea what that did to me?" Clenching my jaw, I tried to rein in my hurt and bitterness, but it couldn't be done. Every bit of betrayal I'd felt all those years ago when she left with no explanation came rushing back, right along with the all-consuming hurt that followed after I discovered she'd kept my daughter from me for over twenty-five years. It was too much. "Twenty-five years I've missed with her. Three years without my granddaughter. That's time I will never get back!"

"Gus, you have to understand. I did what I thought was best for all of us. I was trying to protect you, and when I found out I was pregnant, my parents pushed me to marry Denis. He knew I didn't love him, but because he thought so much of my father, he went along with my mother's wishes … pretended that August was his own." Her voice grew soft as she told me, "We had a good life, but he always knew my heart belonged to another. That never changed, and when my parents died, his commitment to me died along with them."

"And yet, you still didn't come to me. You kept your secrets all to yourself. You didn't even tell August the truth. Made her think that piece-of-shit Denis Rayburn was her father. You've lied to her all these years, just like you did to me!"

"I know. I know all of this, Gus. I'm so sorry I hurt you. I'm sorry that I lied to her, and I kept you both apart for so long," she cried. "I just didn't know what to do. By the time my parents died, too much time had gone by. I didn't know how I was supposed to tell you. It was easier just to pretend that the lie was real."

"Easier for who? You? Me … August?" I understood that she left to protect me, but I couldn't let go of the fact that she'd kept our child away from me. It was unforgivable. I would've never done that to her, not for any reason. "Exactly, who was it easier for, because where I stand, you were the one who had it easy."

"You might think that, but you're wrong. None of this was easy for me. Every time I looked at August, all I could see was you. Your eyes. Your smile. Your hair. Even your stubborn spirit. These little pieces of you were a constant reminder of what I'd left behind, and I had to see them every day of my life."

"But you still had her. You got to be there … to be a part of her life. Do you have any idea what I would've given to be there? To see how beautiful you looked carrying our child. To watch her grow in your belly. To see her the day she was born? I would've given the world to see that girl grow up, to be a part of her life, but you took that from me. You say you did what you thought was best for all of us, but you were wrong, Samantha. I should've been there. August should've had a father who loved her, not just some fucking fill-in your mother chose."

"And how were you going to be that kind of father to her if you were behind bars? That would've been no kind of life for you or for her. You can blame me all you want, but the truth remains. My mother would've made sure you and your brothers spent your lives in prison if I didn't walk away. *Don't you get that!*"

Her words cut through my heart like a knife. I knew what she was saying was true, but that didn't erase the pain I felt in my gut—the pain I knew I'd feel for years to come. "Maybe, but at least then I would've known the truth. I would've known why you'd left, why you'd kept my child from me. I wouldn't have spent the last twenty-five years thinking that I wasn't what you wanted, that you didn't love me the way I loved you."

"I loved you with all my heart and soul, Gus. I loved you more than I thought was humanly possible, that's why I did what I did! I sacrificed everything … my happiness, my chance at love, the life I wanted, so *you* could have those things. I loved you that much!" She started to sob uncontrollably. Damn. It gutted me to see her so upset. I had to fight the urge to try and console her. A part of me wanted to do just that. I wanted to forgive her for keeping August from me even after her parents died and put this all behind us, but the other side of me knew that wasn't possible—at least not yet. "If you want to tear me down and make me pay for the choices I've made, you can rest easy because I've suffered plenty. I spent my entire life loving a man I couldn't have."

"I don't know what you expect me to say, Samantha."

"I don't want you to say anything, Gus. I just want you to understand why I did what I did. I made my mistakes. I know I did. I know there is so much *wrong* with this whole situation, but I gave up everything for you. I never loved another. Never had more children because I couldn't bear the thought of carrying another man's child. I only wanted you, and I had to spend every day and night knowing that I'd lost you. It was hell, Gus. It still is. I've never stopped loving you. Even now, I still have all those same feelings for you, and I don't know what to do with that. In my mind, I know I can't change what I've done, that we can never go back, but my heart still longs for you."

"Dammit, Samantha." I'd heard enough. I'd been trying with everything I had to keep the shitstorm that was raging inside me under control, but I was losing ground. I needed to get the fuck out of there and clear my head. Without looking at her, I charged for the door and said, "I can't do this. I just can't."

When I stepped out in the hall, I took in a deep breath, hoping to collect myself only to find August standing there. It was clear from the expression on her face that she'd heard our conversation. I stepped towards her, but she held up her hand, stopping me in my tracks. "I'm sorry, Gus, but I can't talk about this right now. It's all too much. I need some time to wrap my head around it."

Having no other choice, I nodded and said, "I'm here whenever you're ready."

With that, I turned and walked away, leaving her crying in the hallway. It gutted me to see her hurting like that, especially since I understood the pain she was feeling, but I hoped in time she'd be willing to talk to me about everything that had happened. I hoped we both would.

SAMANTHA

*I*t's amazing how time has a way of changing a person. When I was younger, I felt so full of life. I was driven and confident, secure in my own skin, but with each heartbreak, with each of life's little injustices, a piece of me broke. Over the years, I changed. I lost that spark that burned inside of me and was simply a shell of what I used to be. The same didn't hold true for Gus. Instead, he was everything he used to be and more. When he walked into the room, everyone took notice—everyone. Power and confidence radiated off of him like no man I'd ever known before. His body was thicker, fuller and even more muscular than it was when we were younger, and with his salt and pepper hair, he looked so unbelievably sexy. Of all the changes in him, the one I noticed the most was that fierce look in his eyes. I was a little jealous of that look—the one that implied that life had thrown its punches, but he'd remained standing. He hadn't let it defeat him the way it had me.

I'd spent so many sleepless nights thinking about what

it would be like if I ever crossed paths with Gus again. Sadly, our encounter was nothing like I'd hoped it would be. He didn't instantly forgive me. He didn't take me in his arms, hold me and kiss me the way he used to. In fact, he wouldn't even look at me, much less forgive me. He was so angry and bitter. I don't know why I thought he might behave differently. I knew Gus. I knew the kind of man he was, and I'd let him down. I'd let us both down.

With a heavy heart, I crawled into bed, and as I stared up at the ceiling, I found myself thinking back to the night I left. It was a night I'd thought about many times over the years. I'd known for days that I would have to leave. My mother had given me a week before she'd release the video to the police. I should've left him right away, but I just couldn't make myself go. It was so hard to think I'd never see him again, especially when I loved him the way I did. I wanted to savor every moment I had with him, and that's exactly what I did–right down to our very last night together.

GUS HAD TAKEN *me on one of our rides out in the country, and we'd stopped at a little creek. I'd laid us out a blanket along the bank, and we were watching the fish swim by as the cool breeze whipped around us. He was sitting close, just like he always did, making me feel like I was the most important thing in the world to him. After tossing a few pebbles into the water, Gus looked over at me with those gorgeous dark eyes of his and said, "You know, we need to start thinking about finding us a place to live."*

I could've told him the truth then, but I wasn't ready for the fairytale to end. "We have plenty of time for all of that. Besides, we have my apartment."

"I want us to have a place that's ours."

"I do, too." I wasn't lying when I told him that. I wanted a home with him, a future with children, and a life we could share together, and it broke my heart that we couldn't have it. "But, we have lots going on right now. You and the club. Me and my job. Maybe right now isn't the best time for us to be worrying about that."

"Maybe not, but it doesn't hurt to talk about it."

"I guess not. I just don't want us to get our hopes up."

"Why not? We're just talking, right?" He smiled as he pushed, "So, just tell me. Where would you like to live?"

"If we were living in a perfect world where everything was just the way we wanted, I'd have to say midtown. Hypothetically speaking, of course."

"Of course." He chuckled as he asked, "And what kind of house would you like to have?"

"I don't know. Anything's fine with me, Gus."

"Oh, no. You're not getting off that easy. Tell me what you'd want."

I leaned back and thought for a moment, then answered, "Okay. Again, this is all a fantasyland kind of thing, but I'd love to have one of those little cottages with the cobblestone fireplaces at the front of the house and a small front porch with stone columns and maybe a rose garden in the back."

"Is that all?"

"Yeah." I leaned a little closer to him, "But, honestly ... as long as I knew you were coming home to me every night, I wouldn't care what kind of house we had."

His expression softened, and before I knew what was happening, his mouth was on mine. Without breaking the kiss, he slipped his arms around my waist and pulled me into his lap. I whimpered softly when his tongue delved deeper into my mouth. Shamelessly filled with desire, I wound my arms around his neck and shifted my position. Once I was facing him, I carefully straddled my knees at his sides. His hands slipped under my t-shirt, roaming possessively over my body as he deepened the kiss. I loved how he made me feel so wanted, so desired. We were both quickly getting carried away, forgetting that we were out in broad daylight, until a car drove by only a few yards away. While I found it doubtful that they could see anything, Gus pulled back from our embrace and said, "It's time to go."

"What?" I gasped. "I thought we had all afternoon."

"We did." He eased me off of him and quickly started to stand. Once he was on his feet, he extended his hand to me and said, "But, then you went and kissed me like that, and now, we have to go."

"We do?"

As he pulled me to my feet, he answered, "Yeah, we do."

"Why's that?" I teased.

"Cause I need to bury myself inside my woman, and I have no intention of doing that out here where God and anyone else can see." He placed his hands on my hips and pulled me close. "What you have going on is for my eyes only."

"Oh."

"Now, get that smokin' hot ass of yours on that bike," he ordered with the sexiest smirk I'd ever seen. I nodded, grabbed the blanket off the ground, and rushed over to his motorcycle. I was about to put on my helmet when Gus came up to me and said, "You know what?"

"What?"

"I'm pretty crazy about you."

I'd heard him say those words to me many times, but there was something in his tone that made my chest tighten, like a hot dagger had just impaled my heart. My voice trembled as I *repeated his words back to him. "I'm pretty crazy about you, too, Gus."*

We went back to the clubhouse and spent the afternoon making love: at first, fast and filled with desire, and then slow and tender. Gus made us a bite to eat, and it was well after midnight when he finally drifted off to sleep. I'd never gotten the courage to actually tell him about leaving. I'd considered it many times, but always ended up deciding against it. I knew exactly what would happen if I told Gus the truth. He would try to talk me out of leaving, and my mother would send that video to the police. I simply couldn't let that happen. He meant too much to me. Doing the only thing I could, I eased out of bed and wrote him a farewell letter, pleading with him not to come after me. A little part of me died with each word I wrote, and by the time I was done, I was utterly devastated. I tiptoed over to the bed and stared down at him one last time, trying to burn every inch of him into my memory. With tears streaming down my face, I placed the letter next to his pillow and forced myself to walk out of the room.

When I'd left that day, my heart was irreparably broken. I had quickly spiraled into a terrible depression. I couldn't eat. I couldn't sleep. And if I had my choice, I would've never gotten out of bed. I would've just laid there in my own misery and just let the darkness consume me. Unfortunately, I was staying with my parents, and my mother wasn't exactly understanding about my state of mind. She'd spend hours lecturing me, going on and on about how ashamed she was of me. When it finally got unbearable to lay there and listen to her, I would get up and go to work. At least there, I could have some peace and quiet. I'd like to say that over time things got easier, but they didn't. Day in and day out, all I could think about was Gus. I missed him terribly, and I just wanted to go back to him. Knowing I'd never see him again broke something inside of me, making me numb and bitter.

I'd been home for just over six weeks when I started feeling nauseous all the time. At first, I thought it was just part of the depression, but then I realized I hadn't gotten my period. After I'd gotten a positive result from a pregnancy test, a wave of hope washed over me. I thought I finally had the one piece of the puzzle I needed to persuade my mother to let me go back home to Gus.

When I rushed into my parents' bedroom, I found her sitting up on her bed reading the paper. I could hear my father in the bathroom taking as shower as I tapped on the door and stepped inside. "Mom?"

She lowered her paper and said, "Well, hello, Samantha. It's nice to see you out of the bed for a change."

"I need to talk to you about something."

"Okay." She put her paper to the side and asked, "What do you have on your mind?"

"Well, I haven't been feeling very well ... I've been really tired and nauseous, so today I decide to ... umm ..."

"Come on, Samantha. Just tell me already."

"Well, I wanted to tell you that I'm pregnant."

She glared at me with a cold, blank expression for several seconds, then said, "It's just one problem after another with you, isn't it?"

"I'm sorry you feel that way. It's not like I intended for this to happen."

"Intentional or not, you'll have to get rid of it, Samantha."

"What?"

"You heard me. There's no way you can have this baby."

"Are you kidding me? You want me to have an abortion?" I gasped. "You want me to kill my baby?"

"Oh, don't be so dramatic, Samantha!" she fussed. "People have abortions every day. It's simply a means to an end, and this thing with you and that man must come to an end."

"No." I clenched my fists at my sides as I shouted, "For as long as I can remember, you have dictated every aspect of my life, Mother. You will not dictate this. I am not going to have an abortion. Not now. Not ever."

"And just what do you think you're going to do?"

"I'll go back to Gus and—"

"That's not an option, and you know it," she interrupted. "I'll give that video to the police before I'll ever let that happen."

"Why can't you just let me live my life?"

"You know why!" she huffed. "Your father's campaign is on the line."

"Of course. The campaign," I grumbled. "That's all that matters to you. My happiness has certainly never meant a damn thing to you."

"I've always wanted the very best for you, Samantha. I've never accepted anything less and never will. I won't apologize for that." She crossed her arms as she sat there studying me for several moments. "If you want to keep this baby, that's fine. Keep it, but you'll need to get married right away. He'll need to be someone suitable. Someone the family can be proud of. Someone who can help you raise this child up in a proper home."

"And who would that be, Mother?"

"Well, I've always thought a lot of Denis Rayburn. I think he would make a wonderful husband and, now, I suppose a great father to your unborn child," she answered proudly.

I cringed at the thought, but if it meant keeping my baby, I would do whatever I had to do. "Fine, but what makes you think he would marry me?"

"He would jump at the chance, darling."

Just as the words left her mouth, my father stepped out of the bathroom. He was in his pajama pants and t-shirt, and his hair was still damp as he started towards the bed. "Who would jump at the chance?"

"Denis." Mom smiled and said, "I think he would be thrilled to have August as his better half. Don't you?"

His eyes narrowed. "What are my girls up to now?"

"Nothing, dear," Mom lied. "We're just talking about possibilities and all that."

"Um-hmm." My father cocked his eyebrow as he said, "I didn't think Samantha cared much for Denis."

"Don't be silly. She's crazy about him. I think we should ask him over for dinner tomorrow night," Mom suggested.

"Oh, really?" Dad looked over to me as he asked, "What do you think of that idea, sweetheart?"

I glanced over at Mom, and when I saw the cold look in her eye, I knew what my answer had to be. "Yeah, I think that sounds great."

"All right then. I'll ask him first thing in the morning."

"Okay." As I turned and headed out of the room, I had to fight back the tears as I mumbled, "Good night."

It turned out that Mom was right. Denis did agree to the marriage. I had no idea why, and honestly, I didn't care. I just wanted the whole thing to be over. We had the wedding at my parents' house with just family and friends, and when it was over, Denis and I went back to his house. We barely even spoke. He helped me put my things in the closet, we put on our pajamas, and got into bed. He rolled over with his back to mine and fell asleep. I cried myself to sleep that night and so many nights after. We spent most nights like that—never talking, never touching, and I was okay with that. I never loved Denis, and he never loved me. We'd had a marriage of convenience, and when my parents died, I was thankful that the marriage ended.

Those memories had haunted me for years. There was no way I could ever truly explain to Gus how hard it had been for me. That didn't excuse the fact that I hadn't come to him when my parents died. Every time I would muster up the courage to call him, I would talk myself out of it. I was afraid that he'd just end up hating me for keeping his daughter from him, on top of already hating me for leaving, and I didn't have the strength to handle it—any of it. I knew it was wrong, just like I knew it was wrong not to talk to him the night I left that note, and yet, I still didn't pick up the phone. Instead, I waited, praying that one day I'd find a way to tell him the truth. I guess, in a way, I finally did.

GUS

I spent the entire night going over everything Samantha had told me, trying my best to make sense of it all. Even though I believed her when she said she'd done it all to protect me, I was still having a hard time swallowing it—partly because I felt guilty for the part I played in it all. If I'd been more careful, if I'd been paying more attention and watching my back, then I'd have known that someone was watching us. That way her mother wouldn't have had the means to blackmail her like she did. Because of the mistakes I made, Samantha was forced to make an impossible decision. I wasn't so sure I wouldn't have done the same if I were in her shoes. Hell, I would've done anything to protect her. While I had my doubts that there was anything I could've done to fix the situation, I wished I would've had a chance to set things right. At least then I wouldn't have spent the last twenty-five years wondering why she'd just walked away. Unfortunately, there was nothing I could do to change the past. I could only move forward. It was the only thing any of us could do.

With that in mind, I got up the next morning and met with Viper and the others. Riggs and Hammer were able to hack into all of Polito's security systems, but there was one hitch. The cameras at the house weren't showing us anything—just the view of the outside. Before we could move forward with the plan, Riggs would have to get us eyes inside that house. He felt certain that he could resolve the issue without a great deal of trouble, but he'd need some help. Knowing they could help him get the job done, I sent Murphy and Gunner to Polito's place with Riggs.

Once they were gone, we all continued to discuss the plan of attack. After we got everything sorted, the rest of the brothers started to disperse, leaving Viper and me alone at the conference table. I was surprised when he looked over to me and said, "That Riggs kid is something else."

"Yeah, he is," I answered with pride. Each of my boys brought something special to the club, but Riggs could do shit that blew my mind. I don't know how he pulled off the things he did. I was just glad the boy was on my side of the fucking fence, cause I sure as hell wouldn't want it the other way around. "I'm lucky to have him."

"You've got a great group of brothers. You should be proud."

"I am." My chest tightened as I said, "I've made my mistakes over the years, more than I care to say, but choosing these boys as my brothers wasn't one of them."

"I got this nephew. His name's Clay." His expression grew serious as he continued, "He's a good kid, but he got tangled up with the wrong crew. His mother has tried to get him on the right track, but his old man was killed in a trucking accident a few years back and it's been rough on them all."

"Hate to hear that. There anything I can do?"

"I was wondering if you'd consider letting him come down to Memphis and hang with y'all for a bit. That way he'd get a feel for the club life, and if you think he's got what it takes to be one of your Fury boys, maybe he could prospect for ya."

His voice was strained, letting me know that it wasn't easy for him to ask such a favor. I figured the kid must've been pretty special to him or he wouldn't have asked. "Why not have him prospect for you?"

"The kid needs a fresh start, brother. Too much shit holding him back here."

"How old is he?"

"He's twenty-two but looks closer to thirty." He shook his head as he continued, "He's a mountain of a kid. Six-seven and about two-eighty. He's got a beard thicker than mine."

"You think he'll be up for coming down to Memphis?"

"Absolutely."

"Okay, then. Send him on." I looked him right in the eye as I said, "But ya gotta know, I'm not making any promises here, brother. It's up to Clay whether or not this things works."

"Completely understood. Send his ass right back if he don't fall in line."

"That I'll do." I chuckled as I stood. "I've got something I need to tend to, but it shouldn't take long. If anything comes up, just give me a call."

"You got it."

I walked out of the room, and when I stepped into the hall, I was surprised to see August talking to Hawk, the Sinners' sergeant-at-arms. I might've been concerned that he was making another play, but Gunner had already had words with him. Gunner might seem like a nice guy and all, but Hawk would be a fool to go up against him. As I continued down the hall, I called out to her.

"August?" She whipped around, and it was clear from her expression that I'd caught her off guard. "I was hoping you'd be around."

"Oh, yeah?"

"Wondered if you had a few minutes for us to talk?"

Her voice trembled. "Now?"

"Unless you've got somewhere else you need to be?"

"No. Mom is watching Harper, so I don't have anywhere that I need to be, at least not for a little while." She shrugged with a nervous smile. "So, yeah. I guess I'm free to talk."

"Good." I motioned for her to follow. "Let's find a place where we can talk privately."

I led her out of the clubhouse and out into the parking lot. When we got over to my bike, she gasped, "Wait … You're wanting me to ride on that?"

"Yeah." The look of horror mixed with excitement got to me, and I had to fight back my smile. "Haven't you ever been on a motorcycle before?"

"No, not exactly."

After missing so many of her firsts, it was nice to know that I would be able to take my daughter on her first ride. If I had anything to say about it, I'd be taking

Harper on her first ride as well. As I handed her a helmet, I replied, "Well, there's a first time for everything."

While she strapped on her helmet, I put on mine, then helped her ease on the bike behind me. Once she was settled, I started up the engine. August was stiff as board and clinging to me with all her might when we pulled out of the parking lot, but after twenty minutes or so, her grip loosened and I could feel the tension in her muscles start to relax. I could've gone somewhere close, but I wanted her first ride to be something she could remember. And I also wanted to enjoy the moment with my daughter, so I went on out to Radnor Lake State Park. It was a place I always liked to ride whenever I was in Nashville, and I hoped that August would enjoy the views of the lake. After I found a spot to park, we headed over to a small picnic table by the water and sat down.

I looked over at her, and I was overcome with emotion. I couldn't take any credit for it, but August was a good person with a heart of gold—a daughter that any man would be proud of. Knowing she was my daughter, that she was part of my own flesh and blood, made my heart swell with pride. The thought choked me up, making my voice strained as I told her, "I have so many things I want to say to you, but I don't have a clue where to start."

"I know. I feel the same way." She inhaled a deep breath then said, "I wish things could've been different ... that you didn't have to find out about me like this."

"We both know Samantha had her reasons for keeping you from me, and I'm trying to come to terms with those." I thought back to the damn video tape, and my stomach twisted into a knot. August had overheard the conversation between Samantha and me, so in my mind, she'd already heard too much. I wasn't going to delve deeper into that rabbit hole, but I wanted her to know that I felt guilty for the part I played in things. "I just can't stop thinking about how different things could've been if I'd just followed my gut and had gone after her."

"Why didn't you?"

I reached into my pocket and took out my wallet, pulling out the letter her mother had written me all those years ago. I'd carried it with me since the day she left, and I'd read it more times than I could count. I carefully opened it up and offered her the worn piece of paper. Her eyes widened as she glanced down at the paper and saw that it was from her mother. As I watched her read it, I thought back to the words Samantha had written. I'd read it so many times I'd memorized it by heart.

AUGUST 19, 1994

GUS,

I've been lying here watching you sleep for hours, just thinking about the time we've shared together. This summer has been the best few months of my life. I can honestly say I've never been happier, and that's all because of you. I love you, Gus. I love you with every fiber of my being. You mean so much to me, more than I thought possible. With you, I've learned how it feels to truly love and to be loved. That's why this letter is so hard to write.

I've done a lot of thinking over the past few weeks, and I've come to realize that it doesn't matter how much I love you or you love me. It just isn't enough. We're from two different worlds, headed down two completely different paths, and if we stay together, we're only going to end up destroying one another. I can't bear for that to happen. I love you too much. It breaks my heart to say this to you, but I'm leaving Memphis. I am asking you to please respect my decision. Don't try to find me. Don't call me. Let me find a way to move on, and I will do the same for you. It's the only way either of us will ever make it through this.

This wasn't an easy decision for me. In fact, it's killing me to walk away from you, but deep down I know it's the right thing to do. Please remember—I love you today, I loved you yesterday, and I will love you tomorrow and always. That will never change.

LOVE,

Samantha

THE FIRST TIME I read that letter, I was in shock. I couldn't believe that she'd really left, but as the days passed and she hadn't returned, it slowly started to sink in. I read the letter again and again, each time becoming more and more resentful and angry. I'd thought she'd just blown me off like some summer fucking fling. Sure, I read the letter, but I wasn't hearing what she was trying to say. I was too blinded by my own pride to actually realize that she was trying to tell me something wasn't right. I wasn't sure I really ever understood just how much she was truly hurting until I read it once again last night. I hated that I'd been so damn blind. When August finished reading the letter, she looked up at me with tears streaming down her beautiful face. "Oh, Gus."

"I bet I've read that letter a million times over the years." Unable to look her in the eye, I turned and looked out at the water. That letter had held so much meaning for me over the years, and to find out that I'd gotten it wrong, ripped at me like nothing I'd ever felt before. The sounds of the waves crashing against the bank helped distract me from the tightness I felt building in my throat. "Now, it finally makes sense why she didn't come back to me."

"You really did love her, didn't you?"

"I did. I think I always will." I hadn't exactly been celibate over the past twenty-five years. I'd spent time with a couple of the hang-arounds from time to time, even dated a woman from up north for a couple of months, but nothing with them ever lasted. My heart simply wasn't in it. There was only one woman I wanted, and I wouldn't commit myself to any other. It wouldn't be fair to either of us if I did. I glanced back over to August as I told her, "I tried to move on, tried to forget about the time we had together, but in all my years of searching, I never found anyone who made me feel the way she did."

"So, you never married?"

"Never." I shook my head and shrugged. "Didn't seem right to tie myself to someone who I couldn't truly give my heart to."

After studying me for a moment, her lips curled into a warm smile. "I can see why she loved you so much."

It was hard to believe that I could actually love someone that I'd just met, but there I sat, staring at my beautiful daughter, and there was no doubt in my mind that I loved her. Hell, I'd move heaven and earth for her and Harper. "I want you to know that if I had known about you, I would've—"

"I know, Gus," she interrupted. "And so would I, but we can't go back. We've just gotta find a way to move forward from this. *We all do.*"

I knew she was right. There were so many things I wanted to change, but it couldn't be done. We just had to find a way to accept things the way they were and find a way to make the best of it. I just wasn't sure how. "You got any idea how we do that?"

"No, but I'm sure we can figure it out."

"I certainly hope so." In the little time I'd known her, August had proven herself to be a daughter any man could be proud to have. She was beautiful and smart, a wonderful mother, and she had grit. Lots of it. I reached out and placed my hand on her arm and said, "You're everything a father could want in a daughter, and I really hope you'll give me a chance to get to know you and Harper better."

"I'd like that." She paused for a moment, then winced as she asked, "What about Mom? Do you think you could forgive her? That you two could find a way to work past all this?"

"I'd like to say we could, but I honestly don't know." Forgiveness wasn't something I was good at. When I felt I'd been wronged in some way, I held a grudge, a hard one, and this was no different. The anger and hurt still felt too fresh, and I wasn't sure I had it in me to forgive Samantha. I glanced back over at the lake as I answered, "There's been so much hurt, years and years of it, and not just for me. Samantha endured plenty of heartache of her own. I just don't know how we move on from that."

"If you both still love each other like you say you do, then you'll find a way."

"I guess only time will tell." I wanted to tell her that everything would be okay, that Samantha and I would get through this, but I wasn't so sure. I glanced down at my watch and was surprised how late it had gotten. Riggs and the others would be getting back soon, so I looked over to her and said, "We better be getting back. I need to help get things prepared."

"Prepared for what?"

"Can't say." Hoping that Gunner had talked to her about how things worked in the club, I told her, "That's club business."

"So, you don't discuss club business?"

"No, not with anyone except the brothers."

"Not even with the president's daughter?" A knowing smile spread across her face as she said, "Besides, something tells me that this particular business has something to do with me."

"That might be true, but it doesn't change anything." While I was pleased to know that Gunner had, in fact, spoken with her, I needed her to know that I had my reasons for not talking to her about club business. It was a rule I'd always held on to, and I wasn't about to waver on that decision. "Discussing details only puts you and Harper in danger, August. Not going to let that happen."

"Okay, I understand."

As we started towards my Harley, I looked over my shoulder and said, "I'm guessing since you mentioned the president's daughter thing, that you and Gunner had a conversation."

"We did. In fact, we had a lengthy conversation." She slipped on her helmet, and as she got on behind me, she continued, "In case you didn't know, he really thinks a lot of you."

"I think a lot of him as well." I put on my helmet, and before starting the engine, I told her, "You got yourself a good one with him."

I fired up my bike, then slowly pulled out of the parking spot. Moments later, we were on our way back to the Sinners' clubhouse. We hadn't been riding long when I caught a glimpse of August in my rearview mirror, and she was smiling ear to ear. Just seeing her so happy did my heart good. From where I was sitting, it seemed the tides of change had returned, and they were bringing back what had been mine all along.

SAMANTHA

I'd been watching Harper play with several of her new little friends in the playroom for several hours when she came over and crawled into my lap. The minute she laid her head on my shoulder, I knew it was time for her nap. She didn't even argue when I picked her up and carried her back down to her room. After I got Harper settled in bed, I crawled in next to her and laid my head down on the pillow. I loved these quiet moments with her. It reminded me of the times I'd spent with her mother when she was little. Guilt washed over me when I thought about Gus. He'd missed out on all of those little moments with his daughter and granddaughter. He'd missed those moments because of me. They all had. I could feel the tears stinging my eyes when I heard Harper ask, "You 'tad?"

I quickly wiped the tears from my eyes as I answered, "Yeah. Just a little."

"I t'orry."

"It's okay. I'll be better soon."

She looked up at me with those little, puppy-dog eyes as she said, "I sa'ad, too."

"You are? Why are you sad, sweetheart?"

"I miss fwoppsie. I 'ant 'er back."

Floppsie was her favorite stuffed animal. She carried it around everywhere she went like a little security blanket. We were in such a rush when we left August's house, we accidentally left it behind. From day one, Harper had been begging for her precious toy, especially when she was tired and ready for bed. I hated seeing her upset. It seemed so unfair that she was going through all this, especially because of her father. I wanted to do something to make her feel better. At least then I would feel like I'd done something right—something that actually helped someone I cared about instead of hurting them. I pulled her close as I kissed her on the forehead. "I know you miss Floppsie, and it won't be long until you have her back."

"I 'ant 'er now."

"I know you do. I want you to have her, too." Her brows furrowed and her lips pursed into a pout, and it wasn't long before she started to cry. Her little sniffles tugged at my heart, and I just couldn't stand it a moment longer. "I want you to stay right here for just a minute. Can you do that?"

She nodded with another little sniffle.

I eased out of bed and walked over to the door. When I opened it, I was relieved to see that one of the Sinners was walking down the hall. "Hi. Do you have any idea where Jae might be?"

He smiled as he answered, "Yeah. I just saw her in the kitchen. Do you need me to go get her for you?"

"That would be wonderful. Thank you so much."

"No problem."

Jae had sat with Harper several times, and Harper just adored her. I hoped that she wouldn't mind staying with her for a little while. I waited for her to come to the room and went over to the desk and wrote August a note, letting her know that I was going to the house to get Floppsie. I knew I was taking a big risk, but I couldn't just sit there and do nothing—not anymore. It was time for me to do my part to set things right. Just as I was finishing my note to August, there was a knock at the door. I quickly opened it and found Jae standing in the hall. "Hi, Jae. I really hate to ask again, but would you mind sitting with Harper for a little while? I have a little something I need to take care of."

"Of course, and please don't feel bad about asking." She smiled as she told me, "I love hanging out with her."

"You are such a doll. Thank you." I walked over to Harper and gave her a quick kiss. "I'll be back soon. You get a good nap while I'm gone."

"Twer' you goin'?"

"Just to run a quick errand. I'll be right back."

"I 'ant go wit' you."

"You need to get your nap, sweetie. We'll do something fun when I get back."

She nodded as Jae came over and sat down next to her. As I started towards the door, I realized that I had no idea where the Sinners clubhouse was located. Hoping I wouldn't make her suspicious, I looked over to Jae and said, "Oh, I was wanting to ask … if I was going to have something delivered here, what address would I need to use?"

"329 Clairmont Drive."

"Great. Thanks." Before I walked out of the room, I told her, "I left a note for August on the desk."

"Okay. I'll be sure she gets it."

I closed the door and went across the hall to my room. I took the phone that Gunner had given me and used it to log into my Uber account. Once I'd plugged in the address and confirmed my driver, I laid the phone on the desk and then changed my clothes. As soon as I was dressed, I eased out into the hall and was pleased to see that no one was around. I rushed to the side exit and slipped out into the parking lot. Just as I expected, there was a man standing at the main gate where my Uber would be picking me up. I knew there was only one way I was getting out of there without a hassle. I would have to put on quite a performance and make him believe that I wasn't doing anything wrong. With my shoulders back and my head held high, I made my way over to him and said, "Have you seen my driver?"

The young man looked at me like I had three heads as he asked, "Your what?"

"My *driver*," I repeated louder this time. "He's supposed to be here by now."

"Your driver?" he asked, sounding confused. "Why you need a driver?"

Trying to kept my little act going, I rolled my eyes with annoyance and sighed. "So, I can get where I'm *going*."

"Umm, Ma'am, I don't think you're supposed to be leaving. At least not alone. You guys are under lockdown."

"What's your name, kid?"

"They call me Bolt."

"Now, Bolt. Do you really think I'd be out here asking you about my Uber driver if I wasn't supposed to be leaving?" I asked with sarcasm.

"Well, no ma'am, but I should check with Viper and make sure it's okay."

"Oh, I don't think that's a smart move there, Bolt. He's in the conference room with the guys," I lied. "I'd really hate for a prospect like yourself to get him all riled up by disturbing him over something like this."

"But …"

Just as he started to stammer, my driver pulled up. I gave him a quick pat on the shoulder as I said, "Now, don't you worry. I'll be back in a flash."

Before he could stop me, I eased through the gate and jumped into the backseat of the car. Seconds later, I was on my way to August's. I could hear that little voice in my head screaming at me, telling me that I was making a huge mistake, that I needed to go back to the clubhouse, but I didn't listen. Somehow, I managed to convince myself that I could actually pull this whole thing off. I'd already gotten through the gate. I let myself believe that was the hard part, and the rest should be a breeze. I just needed to get into the house without being seen.

I thought back to the day that Polito's men came to August's house. When Gunner realized that they'd come for August, he had led us all out the backdoor and into her backyard. At first, I had no idea what he was doing, but then he had us slip through a couple of broken slats in the fence and into her neighbor's yard. From there, we were able to get away without being seen. Hoping I could do the same, I instructed the driver to take me to the street behind her house. Once he was parked, I asked for him to wait until I returned. I got out and rushed towards the fence. After I slipped through the broken slats, I made my way to her backdoor. My heart was pounding as I eased it open and stepped inside. The house was a bit of a mess. Chairs were knocked over and lamps were lying on the ground, but it didn't look like anything was broken. As I started towards the living room, I picked up a few things along the way. I'd just placed one of the lamps back on the side table when I noticed Floppsie sitting on the sofa. Feeling like I'd just won the lottery, I rushed over to grab it. Just as I was about to reach for it, I heard something move behind me. Before I could react, I felt something slam against the back of my head, and then everything went black.

It was official. I'd just become *that girl*—the girl who did something stupid and put herself and everyone else in even more danger. To make matters worse, I'd done it for a stuffed rabbit. Damn. I just couldn't win.

GUS

*A*fter August and I returned from our ride, I went
to the conference room to check in with Riggs
and the others. When I walked in, they were all sitting at
the table with Viper talking as they stared at Riggs's
laptop. I went over to see what was going on and was
pleased that they'd managed to get the cameras up and
rolling at Polito's house. As soon as I sat down, they
started filling me in on how they'd set off a neighbor's
security alarm as a distraction, enabling them to get close
enough to the house to set up the cameras. We were
making note of the main entrances and exits when
Gunner came into the room. His eyes were wide with
worry as he said, "We've got a problem."

"What's going on?"

"It's *Samantha*. She's left the clubhouse."

I heard what he'd said, but it just didn't click. There
was no way she could've just gone without someone
knowing, not with all the brothers around. "What the
fuck are you talking about?"

"Samantha left August a note saying she was going to the house to get something for Harper." Gunner looked over to August, and from the look on her face, she was just as shocked as I was. "August has looked for her, but she's nowhere to be found."

"Damn it!" Unable to control my rage, I stood up and shouted, "How the hell did she get out of the fucking gate?"

"I don't know, but I'm sure as hell gonna find out!" Viper was clearly pissed as he turned to Hawk and asked, "Who's monitoring the fucking gate?"

"Bolt's on duty until midnight."

As soon as the words left Hawk's mouth, Viper's face grew red with fury. He slammed his fist down on the table as he ordered, "Get his ass in here, now!"

The room fell silent as Hawk rushed out of the room. My mind was racing a mile a minute, making it difficult to come up with a clear thought. Polito would have men watching August's place, so if Samantha showed up there, I had no doubt that they'd take her. I needed to be sure where she was, so I turned to Riggs and asked, "Can you trace her burner?"

Before he could answer, Gunner announced, "There's no point in trying to trace it. She left it on her desk."

"Well, damn."

"What are we going to do now?" August asked with panic in her voice. "What if those men have her? What if they hurt her?"

"I know you're worried, but we'll find her, August." Gunner reached for her, pulling her close as he assured her, "*We'll find her.*"

116

The second Hawk returned with Bolt, Viper started laying into him, "Were you watching the gate today?"

"Been standing at my post since two this afternoon," Bolt answered.

"Did you happen to see Mrs. Rayburn leave the premises?"

"Yes, sir. I did. She left around five or so," Bolt answered timidly.

Viper took a charging step towards him and grabbed the collar of his t-shirt, fisting it in his hand as he yanked him forward. "And you just let her walk out of here!"

"She told me that she got the okay, Prez." The kid was clearly freaked out as he continued, "I just assumed that she was telling me the truth."

"And you didn't think you should check with me before you just let her waltz out of here!"

"Like I told ya … I-I thought she was telling the truth, sir," the boy stammered. "Under the circumstances, I didn't think she'd make that shit up."

"Goddamn it! How could you be so fucking stupid!" Viper released his hold on him and pointed towards the door as he shouted, "Get your shit and get the fuck out of here. Your days with the Sinners are done."

"But Prez, it was an honest mistake!"

"I'm no longer *Prez* to you. Now get your ass out of my clubhouse!"

With all the commotion going on between Bolt and Viper, I hadn't noticed that Riggs was busy hammering away at his computer. He winced as he muttered something under his breath and turned his laptop monitor towards me, enabling me to see the screen. "Hey, Gus. You're gonna want to see this."

My blood ran cold when I saw that it was the live feed from Polito's main warehouse. Two men were entering a building with Samantha walking between them. They had her blindfolded with her hands behind her back, and she was struggling to keep her footing as they thrust her into the center of the room. A man slipped a chair behind her and gave her a hard shove, forcing her to sit as they all surrounded her. As I sat there watching her fight against her restraints, it hit me all at once. I'd given my heart to Samantha a long time ago. Never wanted it back. She was the one for me back then, and she was the one for me now. I would've realized that sooner, but I'd let my pride get in the way. Knowing that she was in imminent danger enraged me. I wanted to kill Polito with my own bare hands, and if I got the chance, I would. I was too busy watching Samantha to notice that August had come up behind me. "Oh my god! Mom!"

I whipped around and glared at Gunner. "Get her out of here!"

Once he'd taken her out of the room, I turned to Viper and said, "We've gotta get her out of there."

"I get that, brother, but it's too dangerous to just bust up in there," Viper replied. "We've gotta play this thing out the right way."

"And what exactly is the right way here, Viper? They've got her bound and blindfolded. There's no telling what they'll do to her."

"I wish I knew the right answer, but I don't." He tried to keep his voice calm and steady as he continued, "Polito wants August. Not Samantha. He'll use her to get to her daughter. We can't fall into that trap. We just need to hold back and stick to the plan."

"I don't give a fuck about the goddamn plan!" I roared. "I'm not going to just sit here while Samantha's life is in danger!"

I was about to completely lose it when Murphy suggested, "We could move ahead with the plan we already have. We've worked out all the details. We all know what to do and when to do it. We just need to get the job done sooner rather than later."

"He's right." Gunner stepped forward as he said, "We spent hours going over every detail."

"There's one thing we didn't cover," Blaze announced. "I get that we're dividing up, going into each property simultaneously, and wiping these motherfuckers out at the same time, but after? If we want it to look like Polito dropped off the face of the earth, we can't leave any remains behind."

"Don't worry about the cleanup," Viper answered. "We've got that covered."

"Good." Blaze stood up as he said, "Then, let's do this thing."

If I'd learned anything over the years, it was that nothing ever went exactly as planned. While I wished we had more time to prepare, I knew in my gut that we were running out of time. We needed to get Samantha out of there before Polito did something stupid. Eager to get moving, Viper and I gave the guys the go-ahead to move forward. They quickly dispersed, each doing their part to put our plan into action. Once they'd collected all the necessary ammunition, we each loaded up into the SUVs and started towards our assigned locations. I had Shadow, Rider, and twenty or so others with me and we were headed to the main warehouse while Viper had gone with

Gunner, Murphy, Riggs and four others to Polito's house. Hawk and T-Bone took six with them over to the office, and Blaze, Gauge, and Axel had six with them at the other warehouse. We had every location covered. It was just a matter of hitting each at the exact same time, giving Polito no chance to warn any of his men that they were under attack.

The main warehouse was in an industrial area that was no longer populated, with just a few rundown, empty buildings making it seem like a ghost town as we pulled into the parking lot across the street. Once we were parked, we all got out and the guys followed Shadow and me around the back of the neighboring warehouse. Thankfully, Riggs was able to disable the security cameras, so we only had to worry about the outside guards and the guards at the door as we proceeded forward. When we got closer, Shadow motioned his hand towards the main entrance, making sure we all saw the two men standing guard, then he pointed over to the other two positioned at the left and right of the building. Knowing they would have to be dealt with before we could move any closer, Shadow leaned over to me and said, "I'll get the one on the right."

Chains, one of Viper's boys, came up next to me and whispered, "I'll get the guy on the left."

I nodded as I replied, "I'll get the two up-front."

After we took a moment to attach our silencers, we moved into position. The others waited in the shadows as we each moved forward. When I got close enough, I took my shot, killing the first guy with ease. As soon as his lifeless body dropped to the ground, the second turned to see what had happened. I used that moment of distraction to take my second shot, killing him instantly. I looked over my shoulder and was pleased to see that Shadow and Chains had taken care of the other two guards. Seeing that our path had been cleared, I raised my hand and signaled to the rest of the crew that it was time to make our advance. I glanced over at Shadow and told him, "Let's finish this shit."

"You got it, Prez."

With the brothers behind us, Shadow and I made our way over to the main gate. As soon as everyone was in position, he eased the door open and stepped inside. Once he was certain the coast was clear, he motioned for the rest of us to follow. When we stepped inside the building, I stopped and took a moment to survey the area. The place was old and rundown, with a small office upstairs, and various metal containers scattered around. I hated launching an attack in a warehouse. It was too open. Every sound echoed around the metal walls, and there was little to no cover. Tonight was no different. It was like I was leading my men into the fucking lion's den as we headed deeper inside. Several of Polito's men gathered in the center of the building, and my blood ran hot with rage when I saw that the lion himself was towering over Samantha.

Seeing her in danger like that did something to me. All the past bullshit faded away, and all I could think about was getting the woman who consumed my heart and soul to safety. My entire body tensed when I heard him shout, "You're going to tell me where the fuck she is, or I'm going to put a fucking bullet in your goddamn head!"

"I'm not telling you anything." Her blindfold was gone,

but her hands were still bound behind her back. "Not now. Not ever."

"Is that right?" he scoffed. "Well, I'll tell you this. I can make you talk, and I will. Hell, I'll fuck the answers out of you if I have to. For that matter, every man in this room will take his turn with you, if that's what it takes. But I guarantee, you will tell me where she is. You got that?"

"You're wrong. I don't care what you do to me. There's no way in hell I will ever tell you where she is."

"You stupid cunt."

When he raised his hand to hit her, I saw red. Without thinking of the danger that laid ahead, I started charging towards them, shooting with every step I took. Polito's eyes filled with panic when he saw that I was headed in his direction. Frantic, he turned to his men and shouted, "What the fuck are you waiting for? Get him!"

His order came too late. My guys had already moved into action, and in a matter of seconds, Polito's men were dead. All that were left standing were Polito and his right-hand man, Sal Carbone. I continued forward, and when Polito saw that my sights were set on him, he stepped behind Samantha, placing the barrel of his gun at her temple. Then, and only then, did I stop dead in my tracks. Looking quite pleased with himself, he glared at me and said, "Take another step, and she's dead."

"It's time to give it up, Polito," I snarled. "You're done."

"Maybe so, but if I go, she's going with me."

Samantha's eyes met mine, and when I saw how terrified she looked, I wanted to kill Polito right then and there. I had a clean shot but couldn't take it—not with his gun positioned at Samantha's head. He had the advantage, but there was no way in hell I was going to let him know that. "That's not gonna happen. You'll be dead long before you have a chance to pull that fucking trigger. Step away from her now before this gets any messier than it already is."

"Who the fuck are you anyway?"

"It's a little late for introductions, don't ya think?"

Out of the corner of my eye, I could see Shadow approaching. He was just a few steps away from Polito when he shouted, "Just tell me why the fuck you're here, asshole."

"Because you made the mistake of coming after my daughter, and then you took my woman," I shouted. My throat tightened with fury as I went on, "And nobody fucks with my family. Nobody."

Just as the words came out of my mouth, Sal spotted Shadow and tried to warn his boss. "Anthony! Behind you!"

He started to turn, but he wasn't fast enough. Shadow squeezed the trigger, sending a bullet straight through Polito's head. Before Sal had a chance to move, I shot him twice, sending him flailing backwards. I took a quick glance around the room, and when I saw that the job was done, I went over and knelt down beside Samantha. Her voice trembled as she said, "You came."

"Of course, I came, Samantha." I started to untie her hands as I continued, "No way I was gonna let anything happen to you. You gotta know that."

"After everything that's happened," her eyes dropped to the floor, "I wasn't so sure."

I had so many things I wanted to say to her, but it wasn't the time nor the place. We had to get the hell out of there and back to the clubhouse before someone spotted us. Once I had her untied, I lifted her into my arms and held her close to my chest as I carried her out of the warehouse. I couldn't believe how fucking incredible it felt to have her back in my arms. So incredible that when we got out to the SUV, I didn't want to let her go. I just wanted to stand there and relish in the feeling of her body so close to mine. Unfortunately, that wasn't an option. I needed to get in touch with Viper and see how things had gone over at the house, so I opened the door and placed her inside. "Are you okay? Did they hurt you?"

"No. They didn't touch me. Scared me a little, but I'm not hurt," she answered in barely a mutter.

It gutted me to hear her sound so defeated, making me wish I'd been able to do more to protect her. "I'm sorry we couldn't get here sooner."

"You came just in time."

"Regardless, it's over now." I placed my hand on hers and said, "I have to take care of a couple of things, but I'll be back."

"Okay."

I closed the door to the SUV, then headed back inside with the others. I put a call into Viper, letting him know that all was well on our end, and I was pleased to hear that the same held true for them. The boys and I did one final check of the warehouse, then headed back to the Sinners' clubhouse. As soon as we got there, I took Samantha to see August, and she couldn't have been more excited to see that her mother was back safe and sound. I hated to leave Samantha, but I needed to get back to the others. Besides, she was in good hands with August. I was on my way to the conference room when I spotted Gunner and Riggs coming in through the back door with a young woman I'd never seen before. I walked over to them and asked, "Who's the girl?"

"You remember when Harper was taken … how I told you she mentioned that she was with someone?" I nodded, then Gunner continued, "Well, this is her. This is the Gabriella that Harper told me about."

"You find her at Polito's place?"

"Yeah. She was locked in one of the bedrooms," Gunner answered. "Riggs and I found her."

Gabriella was young, nineteen or twenty, with olive-toned skin and straight, dark hair that flowed down around her shoulders. She was a beautiful girl, but there was something in her eyes that concerned me. "You got a last name?"

"I do, but I think it's best that I keep that to myself for now." She cocked her eyebrow at me as she said, "It's not like I have any idea who you people really are."

"No, but we did just save your hide, kid."

"Maybe so, but I've learned not to trust until trust is proven." She looked me dead in the eye as she told me, "While I appreciate you getting me out of that house and away from Anthony Polito, I'd feel a lot better if we could just keep things on a first name basis for now."

"I'm not sure that's gonna work for me. I know nothing about you."

"All I can tell you is Anthony Polito killed my father. They had a deal that didn't go the way he wanted it to, and he was holding me captive for God knows what." She shrugged. "If you need more than that, I can leave. Not sure where I'll go or what I'll do, but I'll figure it out."

"Damn. You're a stubborn little thing, aren't ya?" I thought back to the conversation I'd had with Gunner about Harper being so shaken up when we got her back from Polito. Poor thing must've been scared out of her mind. I couldn't imagine how much worse it could've been if Gabriella hadn't been there with her. Feeling like I owed the kid something for being there for my grand-daughter, I told her, "You hang with us for the time being. Get some rest, and we'll sort things out in the morning. You good with that?"

"Yeah, I'm good with that."

I turned to Riggs and said, "We need to get her to a room, and maybe a change of clothes."

"Yes, sir. She can have mine for now. I'll crash in the family room or something."

"Appreciate it, brother."

When Riggs started down the hall with her, Gunner turned to me and said, "I'm gonna check in with August."

I nodded. "Bring her to the conference room when you're done."

"Is something wrong?"

"No. Just have a loose end we need to tie up."

"Okay. We'll be there in a few minutes."

When I got to the conference room, Viper was already there with T-Bone and Blaze. They filled me in on how things played out with them at the other warehouse and office, then Viper told me about Billy the Butcher, his cleaner. He and his crew were already working to clean up the mess at the house, and once they were done there, they would head over to the other locations. In a matter of a few hours, there would be no trace of Polito anywhere. Now, we just had David to contend with. He was the root of our problem, and I had every intention of making him pay for putting my girls in danger. That need to take him down was the main reason I'd asked Gunner to bring August to speak to us. I was hoping that she'd be able to give us some insight on how to get him where it hurt.

The room fell silent when they both walked into the conference room. After she sat down next to me, I said, "I'm sure by now you know that Polito has been taken care of."

"I do." I looked around at the others as she said, "I've already said this to Gus, but I want you all to know how much I appreciate what you did tonight. I know you put your lives in danger for us, and I will always be indebted to each and every one of you for doing so."

"Like I already told you, that's what we do. We protect what's ours. That's why we asked you to come down here and talk to us." She'd already been through so much and I hated to add to that, but it was time to put an end to all of this, once and for all. "We have one last matter to contend with."

"Okay. What's that?"

"David." I leaned back in my chair and crossed my arms. "We have to decide what we're going to do about him."

"I honestly don't care what you do to him." There was no missing the look of resentment in her eyes when she said, "I'd kill him myself if I could."

"As much as I would love to put a bullet in that man's head, I don't think that's our best move." There wasn't a man out there who deserved it more, but I knew it wasn't an option. We'd have to find another way. "He's the mayor. There's no way in hell we'll be able to take him out without blowback."

"Okay, then. What do you suggest we do?"

"We gotta get him where it hurts." I already knew the answer when I asked, "What's most important to him?"

"Well, that's easy," she scoffed. "His career."

"Then, we take it from him, but we don't stop there." I wanted to see this guy hit rock bottom. I wanted him to wish we'd just killed him. "We take everything from him, including his freedom."

"That sounds great to me, but how?"

Riggs leaned forward and said, "We were hoping you could help us with that."

"I'll do anything you need me to do."

"We have everything we need to prove that David was taking bribes." Riggs handed her a folder, and as she opened it, he told her, "Each one of those deposits can be tracked back to Polito or Carbone, but not just them. David was in bed with several big names. We just need to get this information into the right hands."

"Why couldn't I simply take it to the police?"

"You gotta remember, we don't know who David has in his pocket," Riggs explained. "We just can't take the chance on this getting brushed under the rug."

"I hadn't thought about that."

Shadow added, "The election is just a couple of months away, right?"

"Yeah?"

"And he's running against that Brent Walker guy?"

"He is."

"All right then. I'm sure he would be very interested to know that the guy he's running against is a crook. Hell, his campaign would be made with information like this. If we can get this folder in his hands, then I'd bet he'll do all the work for us."

"You're absolutely right." A spark of excitement flashed through August's eyes as she said, "I know plenty of people who'd be able to help us out. I'll just need to call in a few favors."

"We were hoping you'd say that." I stood up and before I started out of the room, I told her, "You get the names, and we'll make sure they get everything they need to sink David. If we're lucky, they'll put him behind bars."

After Gunner took August back to her room, he returned to the conference room and we all spent the next few hours monitoring all the police scanners, making sure that no one called in with concerns about a possible break-in. Our goal was to make it look like Polito and Carbone had skipped town and left everything they owned behind, and from where I sat, it looked like we'd pulled it off. It was nearly daylight when we finally got word from Viper's cleaner that the job was done. Knowing the boys were exhausted, I sent them to get some shut eye, telling them that we'd meet back in a few hours.

When we left the conference room, I was feeling pretty damn good with how things were playing out. It wouldn't be long before August would have her life back, and we could all put this nightmare behind us. As I started down the hall, I found myself drawn towards Samantha's room. It was late. She was more than likely asleep, but I had to see her.

*A*s soon as we got back to the clubhouse, Gus took me to see August. I felt so terrible for making her worry. I should've never gone over to the house. It was a stupid move, and I would always regret putting everyone in jeopardy like I had. Just as I'd finished telling her all about what had happened in the warehouse, Gunner came to let her know that Gus had something he wanted to discuss with her. When they left, I went to the bathroom and took a hot shower. I was exhausted and hoped that it might help me unwind. Unfortunately, that didn't happen. When I got in bed and closed my eyes, I was suddenly pulled back in that warehouse with Polito and his men. I'd never been so terrified in my entire life. When he threatened to do all those vile things to me, I knew he meant every word. I could see it in his eyes. I could hear it in his voice. I thought for sure that I was going to die in that room, alone and scared, but then I saw Gus coming towards me. It was like something out of a fairytale. My hero had come to save me, but he was no knight in shining armor. Instead, he was a biker—rough, tough, and sexy as hell. When I saw that look in his eye—that look that told me there was still a part of him that cared about me—I thought maybe, just maybe, there was a chance for us after all.

I spent hours tossing and turning, thinking about Gus and how good it felt when he lifted me into his arms. It was a feeling I'd missed more than I realized, and I wanted desperately to have him close again, even if it was just for a brief moment. When I rolled over, I noticed that the sun was starting to rise. I hadn't slept a wink and was considering getting up when I heard a tap at my door. Thinking it might be August, I tossed the covers back and rushed over to answer it. After spending the entire night thinking of him, Gus was there, standing in my doorway looking at me with the same fierceness in his eyes that he had in that warehouse. The air rushed out of my lungs when I heard him say, "I'm sorry if I woke you. I just needed to know you were okay."

"I wasn't sleeping." I stepped back and eased the door open wider. "You want to come in?"

Without answering, he stepped into the room, slowly closing the door behind him as he looked over to me with a serious expression. I had no idea what was going through his head, but the way he was staring at me sent a carnal chill down my spine. I couldn't help but notice that he remained positioned close to the door. He was intentionally keeping his distance, like he was considering his next move. "Why couldn't you sleep?"

"I can't seem to stop thinking about last night." My eyes drifted to the ground as I said, "I'm really sorry. I never should've gone over to the house like that."

"No, you shouldn't have, but what's done is done."

We both just stood there in silence, neither of us really saying what was on our minds, and when I couldn't take it a moment longer, I finally asked, "Do you ever think you'll be able to forgive me for all of this?"

"Which part exactly?"

"All of it. Any of it." I inhaled a deep breath and forced myself to look up at him as I said, "I really hope you'll try."

"I've been trying. It hasn't been easy." He took a step towards me as he said, "You know that saying *Love hurts*?"

"Yes," I nodded.

"That sayings has it all wrong. It's not love that hurts. It's losing someone you care about, missing them so much you can't breathe, that's what fucking hurts." He was just inches away from me when he said, "I could hold onto these fucked up feelings forever, but in the end, I'd only be hurting myself more. I'm done holding grudges."

"Does that mean you forgive me?"

"You know, it's not just you I have to forgive here. I had my own part in all of this, and that's hard for me to swallow."

"I don't understand what you mean."

"If I had been more careful, then your mother would've never had a way to blackmail you like she did. That's on me." My chest tightened when he took another step in my direction, slowly closing the gap between us. "I hope in time I'll find a way to forgive us both."

"And until then?"

"Can't say for sure. We've got things we need to talk about. A trust has been broken, and it will take some time to heal," His eyes met mine as he said, "But the way I see it,

I figure we can both heal a lot faster together than we ever could apart. You get what I'm saying?"

"No. I'm not sure that I do."

"I want you, Samantha. Always have." I gasped when he reached for me, pulling me close to his perfectly defined chest. His lips hovered over mine for several moments, making my entire body tremble with anticipation. "I made the mistake of letting you walk away from me all those years ago. I'm not gonna let that happen again."

Before I could respond, his mouth met mine with a kiss that made my heart race with ecstasy. It was strong, demanding and oh-so possessive, making me want him that much more. Gus was a man who knew what he wanted, and he wasn't afraid to take it. At that moment, he wanted me. His lips traveled down to my neck, teasing me with a trail of feather-light kisses down to my shoulder. Completely consumed in the moment, I whispered his name, over and over. "Oh, Gus."

When his hands dropped to my waist, pulling my hips closer to his, I could feel the growing bulge of his arousal. "You got any idea how much I've missed this?"

I couldn't answer. With his every touch, waves of need jolted through me, every kiss fueling my desire for more, and I was too caught up in the moment to speak. Gus had a way of doing that to me. With just one simple kiss, he could make every nerve in my body come alive. Now was no different. His hands greedily moved under my shirt, caressing my bare breasts. The feeling of his hands on my body lit a spark of desire inside of me, igniting a fire that burned deep within. I inched closer, rocking my hips against him as I tried to chase that feeling. I was quickly losing myself in him when he lowered his mouth to my ear and whispered, "No one has ever gotten to me the way you do, Samantha. No one."

He stepped back, just long enough to slip off his cut, then he was right back on me, kissing me and making me hungry for more. I reached for his cotton t-shirt, carefully pulling it off him. Once it was gone, I took a moment to just look at him. He was a sight to behold, so unbelievably hot, and I couldn't imagine wanting him more than I did at that moment. I was still appreciating the view when his hands dropped to the hem of my t-shirt. He carefully eased it over my head, then tossed it to the side. His eyes slowly roamed over my body, making me suddenly feel insecure. It had been years since he'd seen me this way. I knew I looked quite different, and I feared that he wouldn't find me as attractive as he had when I was younger. Before I realized what I was doing, I wrapped my arms around myself, trying in vain to cover my body. Gus reached for my hands and growled, "Don't try to hide from me, Samantha. I want to see you. All of you."

"But ..."

"You're beautiful. Every fucking inch of you."

Hearing the passion in his voice as he spoke those words gave me the courage to lower my hands. I stood there, feeling the heat of his stare on my body, and I couldn't stop myself from squirming. I'd never felt so wanted, so desired. When the last of his resistance broke, he reached for me, his hands roaming over my bare skin, only stopping when he reached my breasts. I licked my lips in anticipation as he lowered his mouth to my nipple, his tongue flicking across the tip before his lips surrounded it. My breath quickened as he released me from his mouth, and took a step back, eagerly grabbing me by the waist and turning me to face the desk. I felt him twirl his hand around the length of my hair, gently tugging it as he said, "I need inside you. Can't wait a second longer."

A rush of anticipation surged through my body as I leaned forward and placed my palms on the smooth, wooden desk and waited. Goosebumps prickled against my skin when I felt him place his hands on my outer thighs. A small moan echoed through the room as his thumbs hooked in the waist of my lace panties, and he dragged them slowly down to my ankles. As I stepped out of them, I felt his rough fingertips trailing upward between my legs, and my breath caught as fingers found my center, circling my sensitive clit. I heard the clink of his belt buckle and the slide of his zipper, and I groaned while he continued to torment me with his fingers.

Suddenly, I felt his thick erection slide between my legs as one of his hands grabbed my hip. He reached between us and positioned himself at my entrance before thrusting inside me with one hard, smooth stroke. A hiss escaped his lips as my body squeezed around him, adjusting to the fullness. I moaned in pleasure, relishing the feeling of him buried inside of me. His hands reached up to cup my breasts as he began shallow thrusts, readying me. He rolled his hips in an anguishing rhythm as my fingers grasped at the edge of the desk in desperation. His hands moved down to still my hips as he began driving into me with longer, deeper strokes. My body trembled and my breathing became ragged when my climax approached. I gasped as one of his hands reached around to tease my clit. The gentle pressure of his finger overwhelmed me and sent me over the edge.

"Don't stop," I cried while the waves of ecstasy rolled through my body. The pleasure was so intense, my legs momentarily buckled. His strong hands held me upright as my body contracted around his hard cock. His thrusts were relentless as he quickened his pace, chasing his own release. I began to rock my hips back into his, wanting him to be as satisfied as I was. I felt his cock swell inside me when he reached his orgasm. His growl echoed in the room as his rhythm slowed. Moments later, he slowly eased out of me, then bent down and lifted me into his arms, carrying me over to the bed.

He eased down next to me, pulling me close as he told me, "Don't go getting too comfortable. I'm not done with you just yet."

I smiled as I asked, "You're not?"

"Not even close." He leaned towards me as he pressed his lips against mine, kissing me slow and soft. That kiss led into another, and then another. It wasn't long before we were making love again. We took our time, savored every moment, and when we were done, Gus looked over to me and said, "Even better than I remembered."

"Yeah, I think you might be right." I nestled closer to him as I placed my head on his chest. "I've missed you so much."

"Missed you, too. More than you know." He kissed me on the forehead, then said, "As much as I hate to, I've gotta get back to the others. We have a few more things we need to take care of before we head back."

"Head back?"

"Yeah, babe. We've already stayed longer than we

should have." He started to sit up in the bed as he continued, "I need to get back home. See about things there."

I tried to hide my disappointment as I watched him get up and begin putting on his clothes. When he went to put on his cut, I pulled the covers up over me and sat up on the bed. "How soon do you think that will be?"

"A couple of hours. Maybe less."

"That soon?"

"Yeah. We should have things wrapped up here by then." He came over and kissed me, then said, "We'll talk more later. For now, get some rest."

While I had no idea what that talk would entail, I nodded and muttered, "Okay."

And just like that, he walked out of the room and closed the door, leaving me to stew in my thoughts. For a brief moment, I considered doing like Gus had suggested and try to get some rest, but there was no way I was going to be able to sleep. He was leaving. He and the others would be going back to Memphis in a few hours, and I had no idea what that meant for the two of us. I loved him. I'd never stopped loving him. I hated the idea of us being apart. I didn't think I could bear it—not again. With a heavy heart, I got up and went to the bathroom for a hot shower. Once I was done, I put on some fresh clothes and started packing. Seeing that all I had were the things that Gunner had bought for us, it didn't take long for me to gather it all. By the time I was done, August and Harper had returned from getting breakfast, and I went over to help them get ready to go.

We were just finishing up when Gunner came to the door. "Are you guys all set?"

"I guess so." August turned to me as she asked, "Are you ready?"

"As ready as I'll ever be." I started towards the door as I told her, "Let me go grab my things."

I followed August and Harper out to the parking lot. Gunner was loading their things into Hawk's SUV when we walked up. I gave him my bag, then waited as a young woman took a moment to say goodbye to Harper. I'd find out later that she was Gabriella, the woman who'd been locked in that room with my granddaughter. It was clear from Harper's expression that she was sad to see her friend go. Harper never took her eyes off her as she walked over to Riggs's SUV and got inside. As she closed the door behind her, something told me we hadn't seen the last of Gabriella. Once they were done talking, the brothers each came over to send us off. It was hard to say farewell to them, especially after how good they'd been to us, but it was nothing compared to the moment when Gus came over to say his goodbyes.

I was overcome with emotion as I watched him make his way over to August and Harper. It was clear from his expression that it wasn't going to be easy for him to tell his girls goodbye. While I couldn't hear exactly what he was saying, the way he looked at August with such love in his eyes made my heart ache for him. He was such a good man. He'd given our daughter her life back, and I would always be grateful to him for that. He said a few last words to them both, then started walking over to me. I wiped the tears from my eyes and inhaled a deep breath, trying my best to collect myself as he approached. It seemed like we were the only two people in the world as he looked at me and said, "This is going to be harder than I thought."

"I don't want to say goodbye."

"Then don't." He wrapped his arms around me as he pulled me close, hugging me tightly as he whispered, "I'm not going to push you, Samantha. I know you have a life here."

"But what if I don't want that life anymore."

"That's a decision only you can make." He released me from our embrace as he looked down at me and said, "Take your time. Make the right one. I've been waiting for you to come back to me for twenty-five years, Samantha. I can wait a little longer."

"Okay."

He leaned down and gave me a soft kiss, then led me over to the passenger side of the SUV. Once I was inside, he closed the door and headed over to the others. I never took my eyes off of him as Hawk pulled out of the parking lot and onto the main road. I felt as if my heart would shatter into a million pieces when I couldn't see him any longer. Seeing how distraught I was, August suggested that I stay with her for a few days. Even though I didn't want to intrude on her and Gunner, I didn't think I could stand to be alone, so I agreed. When we got to the house, Hawk and Gunner went inside to make sure it was safe. It wasn't long before they returned to let us know that the coast was clear. Since I'd already been to the house, I knew it was a bit of a mess, but with all of us working together, we were able to get things picked up relatively quickly.

As soon as we were done, August got busy unpacking their things while I went into the living room and sat down on the sofa. It didn't take long for my mind to drift to Gus. I thought back to our last few moments together. He wanted me to take my time making a decision about going to Memphis to be with him, but I didn't need time. I knew what I wanted. I wanted a life with him, the life I was meant to have all those years ago. It would take a great deal of courage to pack up and move back there, but when I thought about how good it felt to be in his arms, I knew it would be worth it. I was sitting there and staring at the blank television screen when August came over and sat down next to me. "Are you okay?"

"No, but I will be."

"You'll see him again, Mom."

"I know. I'm just upset with myself for waiting so long to set things straight between us." I'd always known that I loved Gus. I spent years longing for him, crying myself to sleep and praying that it would get easier, and eventually, it did. I was able to let myself push the thoughts of him to the back of my mind, only allowing them to resurface in moments of weakness. I should've never let myself forget. I should've held on to those memories, and maybe they would've given me the strength to go to him years ago. "I've spent so many years wishing things could've been different. I should've done something sooner, and then I wouldn't have wasted so much precious time."

"You can't change what's been done, but you and Gus have a second chance at happiness together." She placed her hand on mine as she told me, "I know he cares a great deal for you, Mom. He's not the kind of man who's just going to let you slip through his fingers again."

I looked over at my daughter, so smart and brave. I'd made my mistakes, but I'd done a good job raising her.

She'd made a good life for herself and her daughter, and now, she had Gunner in her life—a man I knew loved her dearly. She'd found her happiness, and it was time for me to let go and find mine. I knew it might come as a surprise to her, but I was curious to see how she would react when I asked, "Would you think I was crazy if I told you I was thinking of going to Memphis for a while?"

"What do you mean 'for a while'?"

"A few months … just long enough to see if there's anything left of what we had all those years ago?"

A soft smile crossed her face as she answered, "No, I don't think that sounds crazy at all."

"I'm not saying that's something I would actually do, but it's something to think about." I suddenly felt like a weight had been lifted from my shoulders, and I could actually breathe again. A mix of excitement and hope rushed over me as I told her, "I've always loved Memphis, and I have friends there …"

"Mom, it's a good idea. You should do it."

"I think I will."

"Good!" She leaned towards me and gave me a hug as she said, "I want you to be happy, Mom."

"I want the same thing for you." I looked over to the window and watched as Gunner pushed Harper in the swing. He was a handsome boy with a smile that was contagious to all, and it meant the world to me to see how good he was with my girls. "He's a good boy, August, and he's clearly crazy about you and Harper."

"I'm pretty crazy about him too." She stood up and headed towards the door as she said, "I better get out there and give Cade a hand."

"Okay."

141

I stood up and walked over to the window, watching the three of them together. They all looked so happy. Seeing Cade and August together reminded me of Gus and myself when we were younger—so in love, with the world at their fingertips. I would do anything to be able to go back to that point in our lives, but that time had come and gone. While our past was long behind us, there was still hope for our future, and I looked forward to seeing what it would hold for us both.

*L*eaving August and Harper was hard, damn hard, but leaving Samantha was almost unbearable. All the way home, I kept fighting the urge to go back, but then I realized how lucky I was to have something that was so hard to say goodbye to. I tried to hold on to that thought as we made our way back to Memphis. When we finally made it home, I gave the boys the afternoon to get settled in, but that's all I could give them. We had another run coming up, and there were issues that needed to be handled at the garage. Not only that, but we still had to decide what we were going to do about Gabriella, so I told them to all return at six the following morning for church.

Once they all dispersed, I called Moose into my office. After he caught me up to speed on things around the club, I gave him the rundown on everything that had happened when we were gone—how Polito's men had taken Samantha from the house, and how we'd managed to get her back unharmed. As soon as I was done talking, he asked, "So, where's Samantha now?"

"She's at August's place."

"You didn't bring her back with you?" he pushed.

"Moose, *don't start.*"

"I'm not saying a damn thing." He crossed his arms as he leaned back in his chair and stared up at the ceiling. "I'm certainly not going to say that you fucked up by leaving her there."

"Moose," I warned.

"And I'm not gonna say that you're gonna regret it, because you already know that." He looked back over to me and asked, "Don't you?"

"I know that forcing her to do something she's not ready for, isn't the answer. She has to come to me on her own or not at all."

"That didn't work out too well for you the last time."

"The situation was different back then." There was no hiding the aggravation in my tone as I growled, "Besides, there are more important things to discuss than my private life."

"Such as?"

"Such as … *anything else,*" I snapped. "Anything. The club. The garage. Gabriella. Clay. You name it."

"Who the hell is Clay?"

"Viper's nephew. He'll be coming down in a few days." I ran my hand over my beard as I continued, "Apparently, he's gotten himself in some trouble, and Viper was hoping a fresh start might do him some good."

"So, he's going to prospect for us?"

"That will depend on him. I've never laid eyes on the kid." Moose knew better than anyone that I wouldn't let just anyone prospect, so he shouldn't have been surprised when I said, "He'll have to prove himself before I'll even consider it."

His eyes narrowed as he asked, "The boys know he's coming?"

"I haven't mentioned it just yet, but I'll get around to it," I assured him.

"Any idea what you'll do with him when he gets here?"

"I'll set him up in one of the empty rooms … put him to work at either the garage or the restaurant. Something to keep him busy until I get a feel for him."

Moose nodded. "Sounds like a good plan."

I glanced over at the clock and was surprised to see how late it had already gotten. I still needed to unpack and prepare for the following day, so I stood up and told him, "I'm gonna call it a night. I'll see you back here first thing in the morning for church."

"I'll be here." As he started towards the door, he turned back and asked, "Are you at least gonna call her?"

"No. I made my position clear when I left," I answered. "Either she decides to come on her own, or she doesn't come at all."

"And if she does happen to come?"

"Then, I'm never letting her go."

A smile crossed his face. "Now, that's what I wanted to hear."

"I'll see you in the morning."

After Moose left, I went down to my room, put away my things, and took a long hot shower. I crawled into bed and was thankful that I was too exhausted to think. As soon as my head hit the pillow, I was out. The next morning, I woke up well before sunrise. I tried to roll over and catch a few more minutes of sleep, but it was no use. My mind was already racing, and like most mornings, there was no shutting it off. I laid there for a short while, then pulled myself out of bed and got dressed. By the time I made some coffee, checked things in my office, and made a couple of calls, the brothers had started rolling in. I made my way down to the conference room, and as soon as everyone was gathered around the table, I said, "I know we have a lot to cover, but before we get started, I wanted to thank you all for your help with taking down Polito. You went above and beyond to prove your loyalty to me and this club, and I will be forever grateful."

"Nothing we wouldn't do for you, Prez," Riggs replied with sincerity.

"I appreciate that, brother." Knowing I needed to get down to business, I cleared my throat and said, "I talked to Cotton this morning. The run went better than expected, and the payout will be almost double from our previous one."

"Hot damn!" T-Bone roared. "That's what I'm talking about!"

"I thought you'd be pleased." I turned to Blaze as I told him, "Looks like we'll have the funds to hire that custom painter you've been asking for."

"I was hoping you'd say that."

"Any idea who you want to bring in?" I asked.

Blaze shook his head. "Not yet, but I'll ask around and see who's our best option."

"You know, there's that chick down at Thompson's Auto Body who's been doing some pretty cool stuff for them. We might want to check her out," Murphy suggested.

"You talking about Darcy Harrington?" T-Bone asked.

"Yeah. You know anything about her?"

"No, just that she's really something."

"I'll see what I can find out," Blaze assured them. "Hopefully, we can find someone by the end of the week."

"Good. Just let me know what you find out." I turned my attention back to the group as I said, "As some of you know, we brought a guest back with us from Nashville. Her name's Gabriella. Gunner and Riggs found her locked up at Polito's place. Apparently, he killed her father and was keeping her there for one reason or another. I would've left her in Nashville to fend for herself, but she helped out Harper during those days Polito had her. I felt like I owed it to her to help her get back on her feet."

"How you planning on doing that?" Moose asked.

"I'm open for suggestions."

"She could work at the diner," Blaze suggested. "Maybe stay upstairs at that apartment."

"That could work."

"I don't know, Prez," Riggs replied. "We don't have any idea who this girl is. Do we really want her working for us?"

"He's right," Murphy replied. "We got no idea what kind of baggage this girl has brought with her."

"I'm not throwing her out on the street," I barked.

"Then let's see if there's someone else who can take her on." Riggs looked over to Murphy as he asked, "What about Riley's friend ... the guy who owns the bar. You think she could work for him or something?"

"I could ask him and see what he says."

"If we can find her a place to work and a safe place to live, then I'd say our job with her is done."

We discussed a few other club matters, and then it was time for the guys to get to work. As we all stood and started for the door, Murphy came over to me and said, "Riley's birthday is this weekend, and we're all meeting up at Grady's place Friday night to celebrate. It would mean a lot to her if you were there."

"I wouldn't miss it."

"I'll talk to Grady this afternoon and let you know what he says about Gabriella."

I nodded. "I'd appreciate that."

"No problem." When he started out the door, he said, "Friday night at seven! Don't forget."

He was already out the door, so I didn't bother responding. I still had a few things I needed to finish up in my office, but I was in need of another cup of coffee so I headed towards the kitchen first. I'd just passed the family room, when I heard one of the guys call out to me. "Hey, Prez! You're gonna want to see this!"

When I walked into the room, I found several of the brothers standing in front of the television screen. As I stepped closer, I saw that they were watching the news. Once I made my way over to Riggs and Blaze, I asked, "What's going on?"

"It's August's ex." Blaze motioned his head towards the screen. "The cops just arrested him. Looks like there's been an ongoing investigation into him, and their suspicions were confirmed when an anonymous tip came through last night."

"Well, I'll be damned. It worked."

"Sure as hell did," Riggs answered proudly. "They got him for extortion and possible child endangerment."

"Harper?"

"Yep. Looks like he's gonna spend some time behind bars."

I couldn't help but smile as I replied, "Glad to see the asshole got what was coming to him."

"I'm sure August will be pumped about that."

"No doubt." I gave Riggs a pat on the shoulder, then said, "You did good, brother."

We watched the screen for a few minutes longer, then headed out to get busy with our day. After grabbing my coffee, I went back to my office and called Gunner. I wanted to check on how things were going with August. As we expected, she was glad to hear about David's arrest, but wasn't exactly thrilled that Gunner would be heading back the following morning. I could tell from the sound of his voice that he wasn't happy about it either, but he knew going in that it wouldn't be easy. I was tempted to ask him about Samantha. I hadn't heard anything from her since I'd left and wondered how she was doing, but I decided to leave it, thinking it would be best to hear it from her. After I ended the call, I went straight to work. Between preparing for the next run and getting inventory together, I'd barely had a chance to catch my breath, and the following days weren't much better. I was thankful for the distraction. It meant I didn't have time to think about Samantha or the fact that I hadn't heard anything from her since I'd left.

By the time Friday rolled around, I just wanted to have a few beers and call it a night, but that wasn't an option. It was Riley's birthday, and I'd promised Murphy that I'd run by the Smoking Gun—at least for a couple of hours. When I got there, most of the guys were already sitting at the tables with their ol' ladies. I went over and greeted each of the guys, and after I paid my respects to Riley, I grabbed a beer and took a seat next to Blaze, Kenadee, and Riggs. After a few pleasantries, I sat back and listened as they talked amongst themselves. I hadn't been there long, when Gunner came walking up. As expected, they all greeted him by poking fun. He was a good kid, took it all in stride, and just let them have their fun. He was about to sit down next to Riggs when Riley's best friend and cousin, Grady, came walking up with a guy I'd never met before. Grady motioned over to him as he announced, "Hey, guys. For any of you who don't know, this is my brother, Jasper."

I knew the name well. I learned all about him when Riley's father got himself in a mess. Using the connections Jasper had given him, he'd started running guns—something a horse breeder had no business doing. When a deal went bad, we almost lost Riley, but she was a smart girl and managed to get herself out of harm's way. Clearly she wasn't holding a grudge as she smiled and said, "Hey, Jasper. It's been a while."

"Yes, it has."

Sounding almost hopeful, she asked him, "Are you in town for long?"

"Yeah. Madison and I are actually in the process of moving back, but it's going to take some time."

"Madison?"

"It's a long story," Grady interrupted, cutting Jasper off. "I'll tell ya all about it later."

Sensing it wasn't a good time for that particular story, she nodded. "Okay."

Murphy looked over to Grady and said, "I wanted to thank you again for taking on Gabriella. I owe you one."

"Not a problem." Grady pointed in her direction as he said, "She seems to be fitting in just fine."

She was shadowing another young waitress, doing what she could to learn the ropes. I was pleased to see that she was doing okay. I hoped it would stick. Grady lifted his empty beer then announced to all of us, "I think it's time for another round."

"Hell yeah," T-Bone cheered. "Make it two!"

"You got it."

We spent the next hour talking and drinking a few more beers. While it was good to spend time with my boys, I had a lot on my mind and just wanted to head home. I thought I was the only one ready to go until Gunner stood and announced that he was heading out. The guys used the opportunity to give him hell about August.

"He's right. You don't leave a woman like August behind." Blaze shook his head. "She can have a life here, brother."

"So, you're saying I fucked up?"

I'd listened to them go back and forth, but I couldn't hold back a moment longer. I looked over to him as I told him, "That's exactly what he's saying. I can't say that I disagree."

He studied me for a moment, then asked, "You gonna be good with me staying up there for a while?"

"You gonna bring my girls with you when you come back?"

"That's the plan."

I gave him a quick nod as I told him, "Then you have my blessing."

"Thanks, Prez." With a look of determination in his eyes, he started for the door. "I'll be back as soon as I can."

Not long after he was gone, I decided it was time for me to head out as well. I said my goodbyes, then made my way back to the clubhouse. Even though I was tired, I wasn't ready for bed, so I went to the bar for a drink. When I walked in, I found Moose and Rider sitting at the counter taking shots. I walked over, grabbed my favorite bottle of scotch, then sat down next to them. As I poured myself a glass, Moose said, "You're back early."

"I'm getting too old for late nights at the club," I scoffed. "Too fucking crowded and the music is too damn loud."

"You're right. You're getting old," Moose joked. "What about the others? Were they having a good time?"

"Yeah, I'd say so." I shrugged. "Well, Riley seemed to be enjoying herself."

"That's good. Glad to hear it." He downed another shot, then looked over to Rider. "We were thinking about heading over, but by the time we finished stocking supplies, it was already after nine."

"Don't worry." I took a pull from my drink, then said, "With all that was going on, I doubt they missed you."

Our attention was suddenly drawn to the back door when Grinder stuck his head in and shouted, "Hey, Prez. There's some dude here to see you. He said Viper sent him."

Figuring it was his nephew, I told him, "Send him on in."

Seconds later, the door opened wider, and I watched as a man ducked his head down so he could step through the doorframe. When he stood upright, I was surprised to see that he was even bigger than Viper had described. He was at least six-seven, if not taller, with shoulders that were even broader than my own. The kid looked like a fucking lumberjack with his oversized biceps and long, muscular torso. While his size might seem daunting to some, it was the look of indignation in his eyes that concerned me. Grinder led him over to me and said, "This is Gus."

The man extended his hand and said, "I'm Clay. My uncle sent me here to see you."

"Good to meet you, Clay." I shook his hand. "Welcome to the Satan's Fury's clubhouse."

"Thanks. I really appreciate you having me." Something told me he wasn't exactly thrilled about being here, but he was doing his best to hide it. "Viper spoke very highly of you."

"Viper's a good man. He clearly thinks a lot of you. He's hoping you'll get a fresh start here."

Sounding sincere, he replied, "I'm hoping for the same."

"We've got a room set up for you. I'll have Rider show you where it is, and tomorrow we can talk about how you can pull your weight around here."

"Sounds good."

Rider stood and motioned for him to follow as he headed down the hall. Clay hesitated for a brief moment, then followed him out of the bar. As soon as they were gone, I poured myself another glass of scotch. I quickly tossed it back, then placed the empty glass on the counter. Moose looked over to me with a concerned expression as he asked, "You making it all right?"

"I'm fine."

"You sure about that?"

"If you're going to start in on me about Samantha, don't," I warned. "I don't wanna hear it."

"Never understood why you gotta be so damn stubborn."

"Not being stubborn, brother," I argued. "I'm still trying to wrap my head around the shit that went down."

"What's there to wrap your head around?"

"I don't know. Maybe the fact that Samantha never told me about August, even after her folks died," I huffed.

"That's a tough one to swallow, but damn, Gus. Can you imagine the kind of courage it would take to come to you with that kind of news after all those years?" He shook his head as he continued, "It would've been a lot easier to just take that shit to the grave, but she didn't do that. She sent August here, knowing that it would come out that she was your daughter."

"Maybe, but …"

"Enough, brother. Stop making shit so damn difficult," Moose snapped. "You love this woman. Hell, you've always loved her. Stop focusing on the shit you can't change and remember that."

Before I had a chance to respond, Jasmine, one of the club's hang-arounds, walked into the bar. The second she spotted me, she started towards me with a mischievous smile. I knew exactly what she had on her mind as she purred, "Hey there, handsome."

"Jasmine."

She slipped her arms around my neck as she made herself comfortable in my lap. "You up for some company tonight?"

"Thanks, doll, but I'm wiped tonight."

GUS

I realized I should've been more direct when she said, "That's okay. I can help you relax."

"As much as I appreciate the offer, that's not gonna happen."

Before she could respond, Rider came in through the back door and announced, "Hey, Gus. You've got someone here who wants to see you."

"Oh yeah?" I reached for my glass and downed what was left of my drink before I asked, "Who's that?"

Moose nudged me as he looked towards the door. I quickly turned around, and I felt the air rush from my lungs when I saw Samantha standing there. The moment I was hoping for had finally come. The woman I loved had finally found her way back to me, but I had to go and fuck it up by having Jasmine sitting in my lap. I could tell by her pained expression that Samantha was thrown by the sight. Sensing that something was up, Jasmine eased off of me and whispered, "Is that her?"

Caught off-guard by her question, I asked, "Her?"

"Is she the one?"

Then I understood what she meant. Jasmine was a smart girl. While she never had any idea who it was, she'd always known that my heart belonged to another. As I sat there staring at Samantha, I nodded and said, "Yeah, she's the one."

"I thought so. I've never seen you look at anyone like you're looking at her now." There was a slight sadness in her voice as she said, "She must mean a lot to you."

"She does." I didn't take my eyes off of Samantha as I said, "She always has."

"Then, what are you waiting for?" With a warm smile, she gave me a nudge and said, "Go get her."

155

Samantha was still standing by the door when I got up and started walking towards her. I could see the uncertainty in her eyes as she watched me coming towards her, and I'd give anything to take away all of her doubts. When I stood in front of her, I said, "I didn't know you were coming."

"I know. I should've called or something, but," her eyes drifted to the floor, "I just hope I didn't interrupt something or whatever."

"You're kidding me, right?" I reached out and placed the palm of my hand on her cheek, gently forcing her to look at me as I asked, "Do you have any idea how long I've been waiting for you to walk through that door?"

"But …"

"No buts, Samantha. You're the only one I want. You're the only one I've ever wanted." There had always been a fire in Samantha's eyes—one that shined bright, especially when she was looking at me. Seeing her now, I couldn't help but notice that the flame wasn't shining as bright as it used to. Hell, it was practically non-existent, but I had every intention of bringing that flame back. I was going to do everything in my power to make it burn brighter than it ever had. I leaned down and pressed my lips against hers, claiming her with a kiss that was filled with promise. Her mouth was warm and wet, and I immediately got lost in her. I could've stood there kissing her all fucking night. Unfortunately, we weren't alone, so I reluctantly released her from our embrace. "If you can't tell, I'm glad you're here."

A soft smile spread across her face as she replied, "I'm glad I'm here, too."

"Where are your things?"

"I left them in the car." She paused for a moment, then said, "I'm going to look at an apartment in the morning. I was kind of hoping I might be able to crash here until then."

"An apartment? For who?"

"For me," she scoffed. "I'll need a place to stay while I'm here."

"Before you go looking at apartments, I've got something I want to show you."

"Okay." I took her by the hand and led her out into the parking lot. When we got over to my bike, I offered her a helmet. As she slipped it over her head, she asked, "Where are we going?"

"You'll see."

I helped her get on behind me. Once she was settled, I put on my helmet and started up the engine. As I pulled out of the parking lot, she wrapped her arms around me, and I'd never felt anything better. It brought me back to those first rides we'd taken together when she was still terrified of being on a motorcycle. It didn't take her long to figure out that she had nothing to be afraid of. Thankfully, tonight was no different. After a couple of miles, Samantha loosened her grip and her body started to relax. It felt good to have my girl back. Damn good. Now that she was back where she belonged, I had every intention of keeping her here.

SAMANTHA

*A*s much as I wanted to be with Gus and share a life with him, deciding to come to Memphis wasn't an easy decision. It wasn't that I wasn't certain that I wanted to be with him. I did. More than anything, but so much had changed. We weren't the same people we were back then, especially me. I was no longer the strong-willed, confident woman I used to be. Life had sucked her right out of me, and I wasn't sure I had it in me to bring her back—not anymore. The thought terrified me. I knew I would need her if I was going to claim my place in Gus's world. I realized that the second I walked into the club-house bar and found him with one of the club girls sitting in his lap. She was a beautiful, young woman with her arms wrapped around his neck like she was ready to devour him, and the sight of them together made my stomach turn. While he was quick to set things straight with me, assuring me that I was the only woman for him, I needed to have the fortitude and determination to handle situations like that. He was the president of Satan's

Fury, one of the most notorious MCs in the South, and if he was going to be mine, I'd have to become reacquainted with the woman I used to be.

At first, I thought it just wasn't possible, but then Gus told me he had something he wanted to show me. Having no idea what he was talking about, I followed him out to the parking lot. When I got on the back of Gus's bike, I was afraid I wouldn't remember what to do, but I kept my fears to myself and held on. Thankfully, it wasn't long before it all came back to me, and I started to relax and enjoy the ride. I knew I was feeling that way because of Gus. He'd always had a way of bringing out that spark of adventure in me. As I sat there relishing in the feeling of his body so close to mine, I found myself wondering if there were more parts of me that Gus could help bring back to life.

I was lost in my thoughts when Gus pulled up to the most beautiful, little cottage I'd ever seen. There was a cobblestone fireplace outlining the front of the house with a large front porch with the same cobblestone columns. Gorgeous rose bushes were planted on either side of the entry steps with a rustic lamp post positioned at the corner's edge. He turned off the engine, and started to stand before I realized that we'd arrived at our destination. "Where are we?"

As Gus removed his helmet, he said, "You'll see."

He waited as I got off and removed my helmet, then took my hand and led me towards the front of the house. I was completely spellbound as we started up the steps. When he went to unlock the door, I asked, "What are we doing here, Gus?"

"Well, I guess that's up to you." He opened the door

and turned on the lights as he stepped inside. "Come on in and have a look around."

As he walked into the living room, he glanced back over to me, watching my reaction as I followed behind him. I could only imagine my expression as I looked around the room. It was incredible, like the place was made for me. There were hardwood floors with sand-colored walls, and an oversized sofa and chair made for sprawling out on those long Sunday afternoons. The furniture looked like it had been picked right out of a *Southern Living* magazine advertisement, and that was just the living room. Each and every room was equally as gorgeous. I'd just stepped into the kitchen when it hit me. This was the exact house I'd described to him on our last day together. The revelation caused me to stop dead in my tracks. "Gus?"

When I turned to face him, he was leaning against the doorframe with a smirk on his face. "Yeah?"

"Is this your house?"

"No." His eyes met mine as he said, "It's yours."

"What do you mean?"

"I found it a few months after you left."

"So, you just bought it?" I pushed.

"Yeah. I remembered you saying you wanted a place like this." As he started towards me, he said, "So, I bought it."

I was completely floored as I asked, "You bought it just because I wanted a house like this?"

"Yeah." He placed his hands on my hips and said, "I stay here now and then, but always alone. This place has always been yours."

"Gus, I can't believe you did this."

"Well, I did, and now you can stay here instead of some apartment."

It was at that moment that I realized just how much Gus truly cared about me, how he'd always cared for me, and that realization alone sent a rush of warmth through my heart. "I don't deserve you."

"No." He pulled me close as he said, "You deserve a whole lot more than me, but *me* is what you've got."

I wound my arms around his neck and whispered, "You are all I need ... you're all I've ever needed."

The words had barely left my mouth before Gus was on me, kissing me with a passion like I'd never known. My entire body tingled with desire as he delved into my mouth, and it was clear he felt that same desire when his fingers dug into the sides of my waist, pulling me closer to him. His scent enveloped me, an intoxicating mixture of cologne and leather, and I couldn't hold back a moment longer. I slipped my hands under his cut and carefully lowered it down his thick, muscular arms. After laying it down on the counter, I started for his t-shirt, and he bent down as I pulled it over his head. Once it was gone, our hands became frantic, quickly removing the remaining clothes that separated us. In just a few seconds, I was wearing only my lace bra and panties.

My eyes roamed over his body, traveling along the lines and curves of the muscles in his chest, then back to his handsome face. When I saw the way he was staring at me, like a wild animal about to devour its prey, I nearly lost my breath. Without saying a word, he knelt down and lifted me into his arms, then he carried me down the hall to the bedroom. His eyes never left mine as he lowered my feet to the floor.

"Mine," slipped through his lips just before he pulled me in for another heated kiss. His hands slowly eased behind my back to release the clasp of my bra. As the fabric slipped away from my body, I felt his lips glide across my skin to my breast. "Every fucking inch of you, and you'll stay mine until I take my last fucking breath. You got that?"

"Yeah. I got it."

He guided me back onto the mattress as he settled in between my legs. I lifted my hips towards him as I tried desperately to find relief for the burning need that was building up inside me. His eyes locked on mine as his hand slowly slid between us. My breath caught as he traced his fingers across my panties, teasing me with his light caresses before pushing the fabric to the side. He casually slid his fingers inside me, tormenting me with his touch. It had started with just a spark, but it wasn't long before I was consumed with need. That feeling only intensified when his thumb began circling my swollen clit, drawing out my pleasure. It wasn't long before my orgasm took hold, and the muscles in my body started quivering uncontrollably. I was still trying to catch my breath when I felt my panties being slipped down over my hips.

Now completely bare, Gus looked down at me with fire in his eyes as he growled, "So fucking beautiful."

That fire remained in his eyes the entire night as he made love to me, over and over again. It was nearly dawn when we both finally drifted off to sleep. When I woke up the next morning, I was both surprised and disappointed to see that I was in the bed alone. I laid there a few moments, trying to listen for any sign of Gus, but heard nothing. Assuming that he'd already gone to the clubhouse, I got up and went over to his dresser to find something to wear. There wasn't much, but I managed to find an old t-shirt. Once I slipped it on, I made my way into the kitchen. When I walked in, I saw that Gus had left me a note on the counter.

MORNING BEAUTIFUL,

I had to make a run to the clubhouse, but I shouldn't be long. I had the boys bring your car over. I didn't want to wake you, so I put your things in the living room. If you need anything, just give me a call. See you soon.

Gus

Coffee is ready and bagels are in the fridge.

WITH A SMILE ON MY FACE, I returned the note to the counter and made myself a cup of coffee. I carried it into the living room, and just as he'd said, my things were waiting for me by the door. I stopped and just took a moment to look around. I was in complete awe. It was my dream house. While I absolutely loved it, being there saddened me. I couldn't help but think how different my life could've been. If my mother hadn't forced me to walk away from Gus, we could've raised our daughter in this house. We could've lived the life we wanted, and I had no doubt in my mind that we would've been happy—truly happy. I would never be able to forgive my mother for what she'd taken from us, but I found comfort in knowing she hadn't completely succeeded. She wasn't able to keep us apart forever. And she wasn't able to destroy the love we had for each other. We had both carried it with us for all these year, and now, we'd found our way back to each other. From where I stood, our future was looking brighter than ever. I finally had a chance to have the life I wanted with Gus, and I was going to savor every minute of it.

Over the next few weeks, I started to feel more at home in my new surroundings. I had my things put away and started learning my way around town again. I'd even tackled the grocery store, which was no small feat considering that there was nothing in the house to eat and no house supplies. It wasn't surprising. He'd spent most of his time at the clubhouse, so there wasn't a need. That had changed since I'd moved in. He'd go to the clubhouse first thing in the morning, well before the sunrise, and as soon as he was done with his work there, he would come back home to me. We'd spend the night together, talking and sharing our day. Some of those talks had gotten pretty intense. Gus was still working through some things, especially where August was concerned. There were no magic words that I could say to take his hurt away, only time and understanding could do that, but over time, those old wounds started to heal—not just for him, but for me, as well. I was finding my way back to the old Samantha, and I owed it all to Gus. He knew exactly how to fuel the flame that once burned deep inside of me, and with each moment I shared with him, that fire only grew stronger.

I thought it couldn't be possible for things to get any better, but then August called to let us know that she was moving in with Cade. We were both thrilled about the news, and I was tickled that she'd asked us to watch Harper for a couple of days while they packed. August dropped her off first thing in the morning, and Harper was raring to go. She had us running from the second she stepped through the door, and by the end of the day, Gus and I were both exhausted. Hoping to settle her down, we brought her into the living room and put on her favorite movie. As soon as Gus sat down in his recliner, Harper rushed over and climbed in his lap. Gus was wearing one of his white, sleeveless undershirts, and Harper quickly became enthralled with all of his tattoos.

Her brows furrowed as she pointed to one and asked, "Wat 'dis one?"

"That's a motorcycle engine with flames coming out of it," he answered. "I got that one a long time ago."

"And 'dis one?" she asked as she pointed to another.

"That's a skull."

"I no 'ike dat one." Her nose crinkled as she told him, "It skeer me."

"It's nothing to be scared of, sweetheart. It's just a tattoo." He pulled down the collar of his t-shirt, revealing a deep red heart with the word *Forever* scrolled across it. "I got this one after I met your grandmother."

"Why?"

"Cause I knew she would have my heart forever."

A smile spread across her face as she told him, "I 'ike dat one."

Gus looked over to me and said, "I like that one, too."

"I 'ant one."

"You're too young and pretty for a real tattoo, but maybe a temporary one will do the trick." He reached over and grabbed a pen off of the side table, then drew a tiny heart on the inside of Harper's wrist. "How's that?"

She nodded with a smile. "Pwiddy."

"Good."

The movie had been playing for several minutes, but Harper's attention was solely focused on Gus. She reached up and started toying with his beard, taking little sections and twirling them into curls. Gus never complained. Instead, he just leaned back in his chair and let her have her fun. It wasn't long before she had her fill and turned to face the TV, nestling herself in the crook of Gus's arm. A few minutes later, her eyelids started to get heavy, and even though she tried to fight it, she drifted off to sleep. Instead of getting up and putting her in the bed, Gus just sat there, staring at her as she slept in his arms. Seeing the way he looked at her with such love and adoration in his eyes only made me love him more. Gus might've been a tough MC president, who ruled with an iron fist, but there was another side to him. He was loyal and true, he loved without limitations or conditions, and there was nothing in this world he wouldn't do for those he called family.

GUS

*T*hings couldn't have been better. I had my woman back in my arms, my daughter and granddaughter were living just minutes away, and the club was thriving. There was a time when I might've been concerned that things were going too well. I knew there was a chance that something bad was waiting just over the horizon, but I wasn't going to let that stop me from enjoying the here and now. I was going to relish every moment, especially those moments I got to spend with my girls. After spending several days packing up her place in Nashville, Gunner and August had come by the house to pick up Harper. It was clear from their expression they were exhausted but excited about starting their lives together. August and Samantha were helping Harper gather her things while Gunner and I went into the kitchen to grab a drink.

I went over to the fridge and grabbed a couple of beers, and as I offered him one, I asked, "Did you get it all done?"

"We finished boxing everything up late last night." He opened the bottle and took a drink before he said, "I don't think she realized how much stuff they had."

"I don't think anybody really knows until they have to pack it all up." I sat down on one of the kitchen stools as I asked, "Were the prospects any help?"

"Yeah. They're over at the house unloading everything now."

Before I could respond, August walked over to Gunner and took the beer out of his hand. After taking a quick sip, she gave it back to him and said, "Thank you for watching Harper for us."

"No need to thank me. We enjoyed it."

"She did too. She was just telling me what a great time she had with you two." August sat down next to me as she continued, "I don't think she's happy about leaving."

"I can't say I'm all that happy about it either." I shrugged.

"Well, something tells me she'll be around plenty."

"You won't hear any complaints from me." I smiled as I told her, "I kinda like having her around. That goes for her mother, too."

"Seeing that we'll be living just a few miles away, I'd say that's a good thing," August chuckled. "We'll try our best not to wear out our welcome."

"Not possible." I took another drink of my beer before asking, "What do you think of Gunner's place?"

"It's wonderful. Such a beautiful place, and the location couldn't be better. Harper loves it too. She already has her room picked out."

"We've got some work to do. Painting and new flooring, but it shouldn't take long to get things sorted," Gunner added.

"Good. Glad to hear that."

When Harper started fussing in the next room, August let out a small sigh, then said, "I guess I better go and try to wrangle her up."

"You take a break," Gunner told her as he started out of the room. "I'll get her."

"Thank you." Once he'd walked out of the room, August turned her attention back to me. "Mom looks really happy. In fact, I don't think I've ever seen her this happy."

"I have every intention of making sure she stays that way. And the same goes for you. I want you and Harper to have the life you've always wanted, and if there's ever anything I can do to make sure that happens, you just let me know."

"You've already done plenty. Besides, I'm really good." A smile crossed her face as she said, "Cade truly makes me happy, and he makes Harper happy, too. I couldn't ask for more than that."

"Gunner is a good man. He'll do his best to do right by you and Harper."

"I know he will." She reached over and placed her hand on mine as she said, "I'm really glad that we are going to be living closer."

"Me too. More than you know."

We were still sitting there talking when Gunner walked back into the kitchen and said, "Hey, Blaze and Kenadee just pulled up."

"I didn't know they were planning to come by." I stood

up and started for the door. "You know if something's up?"

"I haven't heard anything, but Blaze didn't look happy," Gunner replied as he followed me out to the front porch.

Blaze and Kenadee had never been out to the house, so I had a feeling something was wrong. The second I saw Blaze, I knew I was right. It was written all over his face. The man looked like he'd seen a fucking ghost, and Kenadee didn't look much better. I watched with concern as they got off his Harley and started towards Gunner and me. After they'd greeted us both, Blaze looked over to me and announced, "We've got a problem."

"What's going on?"

"Kenadee was working the graveyard shift last night at the hospital. Things were trucking along like usual when all hell broke loose." Kenadee was a triage nurse at the Regional Hospital ER. She was great at her job, even helped us out when we were in a tight spot, but she hadn't chosen the safest environment to work. That particular ER was known for having a constant stream of gunshot victims, drug overdoses, and worse, but Kenadee felt like she was making a difference by working there. Blaze glanced over at her with a concerned expression as he said, "A kid with several gunshot wounds came in around three this morning."

"He was in pretty rough shape when he got there," Kenadee added. "I knew from the minute I saw his stats that there was a good chance we'd lose him."

It was clear to see that Kenadee was upset about the kid. I could hear the anguish in her voice, but it wasn't like this was the first time she'd had a patient in bad shape. It was Memphis, after all. "I'm sorry to hear about this kid getting shot and all, but I'm not seeing how any of this is a problem for us."

"We're getting to that," Blaze told me. "Kenadee was the lead nurse that night. It was her job to assess the situation and determine what medical needs he might have. He obviously needed emergency surgery, but they had to stabilize him before that could happen."

"Yeah?"

"He'd lost a lot of blood, and his blood pressure was dropping by the second." Kenadee sighed before continuing, "We were doing what we could to get him prepped for surgery when his father came in. He was a scary dude, covered from head to toe with gang tattoos, and he was freaking out over his son being shot. Screaming and throwing stuff around. He was completely losing it."

"I'm guessing that didn't help matters."

"No. Not at all. I'd never seen anything like it." Kenadee ran her fingers through her hair and continued, "I was trying to settle the guy down when his son flat-lined. We called in the crash cart and did everything we could to bring him back, but it was too late. He was already gone."

"Sounds like you did everything possible to save the kid."

"We did, but his father didn't see it that way. He started screaming that we'd done it on purpose, that we'd just let him die because we didn't think he was worth saving, and there was nothing we could say to convince him otherwise. We finally had to call security, and that's when things went from bad to worse."

"What happened?"

"The guy started making all these threats, saying that I

was a murderer and he was going to make me pay for killing his boy. He said he was going to make me wish I was the one who'd died on that table."

"I know this kind of shit happens," Blaze added. "People get upset and say shit they don't mean, but we're talking about Keshawn Lewis, the leader of the Inner Disciples. This guy is no joke."

"Fuck." I reached into my front pocket and took out my pack of cigarettes. After I lit one, I took a long drag, then said, "I don't want us to go buying trouble over this. You were right. People say shit when they're upset. Hopefully, when this guy settles down, he'll see that he was wrong to blame Kenadee."

"And if he doesn't settle down?"

"Then, he'll have to deal with us." I looked over to Blaze as I said, "I've got no idea what this guy will do, so we need to play it safe. I want someone with Kenadee at all times, even when she's at work."

"Agreed."

"Y'all will need to stay at the clubhouse until this blows over. You'll be safer there than anywhere," I ordered.

"We'll get Kevin and head over there now," Blaze replied. "Thanks, Gus. I appreciate your help with this."

"That's what family's for, brother." When they turned to leave, I called out to him, "I'll be over there later to check in with you."

"Sounds good. See you then."

After they'd gotten on Blaze's Harley, they both waved, and moments later, they were pulling out of the drive. Once they were gone, Gunner looked over to me and said, "You think this guy will really go after Kenadee?"

"Hell if I know. People do some fucked-up stuff when tragedy hits." I inhaled a deep breath. "Hoping this asshole will come to his senses and not do anything stupid."

"The Disciples are no joke," Gunner replied with concern. "Going head to head with them will come at a cost."

"Let's hope it doesn't come to that."

Samantha stuck her head out the front door and asked, "Is everything okay?"

"Yeah, everything's fine, or at least it will be," I answered. "Is Harper all packed up?"

"Yes. August is getting her now."

Moments later, August came to the door carrying Harper. "Thank you both again for letting her stay with you."

Gunner took Harper's bag from August's hand as he said, "We owe you one."

"Don't be silly. We loved having her," Samantha fussed. "Now, you three go get settled. If you need any help, just give us a shout."

"Will do."

August gave us both a quick hug, then she and Gunner took Harper over to the SUV. They were about to put her inside when Harper stopped them. August put her down and she rushed over to me. I knelt down beside her and asked, "Did you forget something?"

Without answering, she reached up and wrapped her arms around my neck, hugging me tightly. My heart swelled as I hugged her back. Damn. Never thought a kid could get to me the way she did. She held on to me for several moments, then waved as she rushed back over to the SUV with August and Gunner. "Bye!"

"Bye, kiddo."

Samantha and I stood on the front porch and watched as they pulled out of the driveway. Once they were gone, Samantha slipped her arm through mine and rested her head on my shoulder. "You're really something, Augustus Tanner."

"You think so?"

"I do." She inched closer as she said, "And if you didn't know it already, I happen to love you a lot."

"You do?" I teased.

"Yes. Very much so."

"Enough to marry me?" I asked.

Her eyes widened as she looked up at me and asked, "What?"

"Do you love me enough to marry me?" She didn't respond. Instead, she just stood there staring at me with a stunned expression on her face. So fucking beautiful. I slipped my hand into my pocket and pulled out a diamond engagement ring. I'd been carrying it around for days, hoping the right moment would come along for me to ask her to marry me. While the timing might not have been perfect, I couldn't stand to wait a second longer. "It's a yes or no question, Samantha."

Tears started to fill her eyes as she stared at it and nodded. "Yes. My answer is yes."

"I love you, Samantha. Always have. Always will."

I slipped the ring on her finger, then reached for her, pulling her close as I lowered my mouth to hers. As I stood there kissing her, I thought back to all those years I spent wishing she would find her way back to me. Now that I had her back, there was no way in hell I was ever letting her go. Samantha was mine. Now and forever.

I released her from our embrace, then looked down at her and said, "You sure you wanna get hitched to an old biker like me?"

"Not a doubt in my mind." She looked up at me with a bright smile as she said, "You've just made me a very happy lady."

"Happy enough to make your ol' man some grub?"

"What do you have in mind?"

I ran my hand over my stomach as I continued, "I could sure go for some of that fried chicken you used to make."

"Yeah, I might be able to manage that."

My mouth started to water as I asked, "And some mashed potatoes ... and some of those homemade biscuits?"

She nodded. "Sure."

As we started inside the house, I asked, "Hey, how about an apple pie for dessert?"

"Okay, I can make an apple pie, too."

"That's my girl."

Samantha was about to walk into the kitchen when she stopped and looked over to me. "So, what are you going to be doing while I'm fixing dinner?"

"I'm going to be helping you, of course."

Her lips curled into smile as she said, "You're one of the good ones, Gus Tanner."

"I wouldn't go that far." I gave her a quick slap on the ass as I walked by her and into the kitchen. "I'm helping so we can get to eatin' faster, cause the sooner we eat, the sooner I get my woman in my bed."

"I like your way of thinking."

Just as I'd promised, I helped Samantha make dinner,

and once we were done eating, we let our food settle by watching a little TV. When our movie was over, I carried her to bed and spent the night making love to her. As the days and weeks went by, Samantha and I settled into a familiar routine. We'd wake up together and make love, we'd take turns making breakfast, and then, I would head to the club. Samantha stayed busy with Harper or volunteering at one of the local elementary school. Sometimes, I was able to sneak home and enjoy my woman in the middle of the day. Those were the best days of all. Summer came and went, and when fall finally arrived, I took Samantha away for a weekend. I was ready to make it official, so I made arrangements for us to get married. I'd considered having it be just the two of us, but the more I thought about it, I realized it just wouldn't have been the same without August, Harper, and Gunner being there. As I'd hoped, they agreed to come, and the day couldn't have been more perfect. As we stood there sharing our vows, I found myself thinking about the fateful day when she left. Back then, I never would've imagined that my life would turn out like this, but time has a way of coming full circle. I was right where I wanted to be with the only person I ever wanted to be with.

EPILOGUE

Two Years Later

"Hey, Samantha!" I yelled from the bedroom. I knew she was busy. We were supposed to be leaving for the clubhouse in a few minutes and she was trying to finish getting ready, but that didn't stop me from asking, "Can you come here for a second? I need your help with something."

I could hear her scurrying around the bathroom as she asked, "Help with what?"

"I've got a problem here, and I was hoping you could help me out with it."

"Can it wait a second? I'm almost done getting ready."

"I don't know." I tried to bite back my smile as I said, "I don't think this problem can wait."

"Okay, I'm coming." I was standing at the foot of the bed with a smile on my face and my jeans down around my ankles. The second she stepped into the room, her eyes dropped to my hand as I stroked my hard cock. A spark of hunger flashed through her eyes as she started towards me. "Whoa, that looks like a pretty big problem you've got there."

"It is." I nodded with a smirk. "Not real sure what to do about it."

"Maybe I can help you out."

She took a deep, shuddering breath as the palms of her hands roamed over my bare chest and down towards my abdomen. An appraising look crossed her face as she slowly dropped to her knees. I inhaled a deep breath when I felt her warm hand replace my own. I could feel the heat of her breath against my bare skin as she slowly moved her hand up and down my hard, thick shaft. I was relishing in the sensation when I felt her tongue brush against the tip. My head fell back as she took me into her mouth. The warmth of her mouth and the swirl of her tongue across the tip of my cock made me throb with need.

"Fuck!" She looked up at me with hunger in her eyes as my hands dove into her hair, gripping tightly at the nape of her neck. Her fingers tightened around me as she continued to stroke up and down the length of my shaft. She took me in deep, greedy and needful, and every muscle in my body grew tense. Every flick of her tongue, every twist of her hand, every suck brought me closer to the edge. I wanted to savor the moment, enjoy every second of having my cock buried deep in her mouth, but my dick had other plans. "Fuck, woman. I love your mouth, but I need to be inside you. *Now!*"

Her eyes never left mine as she loosened her grip on

my cock and slowly stood up before me. My hands dropped to her waist as I reached for the hem of her t-shirt, carefully pulling it over her head. Pretending to care, she whispered, "You know we're going to be late."

"I'm the president, Samantha. No one's going to say a damn word about me being late," I told her as I unclasped her bra and slid it down her arms. After I tossed it to the floor, I lowered my mouth to her breasts as I captured one of her nipples in my mouth. A soft whimper filled the room as I ran the tip of my tongue across her sensitive flesh. While I tormented her with my mouth, her hands drifted down to the button of her jeans. Once she had them undone, she quickly lowered them and her lacy panties to the floor and kicked them to the side. She stood there completely bare and beautiful, making my cock throb with anticipation. When I couldn't wait a moment longer, I growled, "Get on the bed."

My voice was deeper, more demanding than I'd intended, but from the look in her eye, I could tell she liked it. She slowly stepped over to the edge of the bed and lowered herself onto the mattress. With her hair draped across her shoulder, she looked absolutely beautiful. I couldn't take my eyes off her as I whispered, "Mine. *All mine.*"

"Yes. I'm all yours," she panted as I settled between her legs. With one hard thrust, I buried myself deep inside her. She felt so fucking good. I wanted to savor the sensation, but I couldn't hold back. I took her hard and fast, and it wasn't long before her orgasm started to take hold. When I felt her clamp down around my cock, I drove into her again and again with a relentless pace. Her nails raked against my back as she screamed out my name, "Gus!"

That's all it took. With one last hard thrust, I found my release, and I came deep inside her. After several seconds, I lowered myself onto the bed next to her with a satisfied smile on my face. Samantha rolled towards me and said, "Looks like your problem is solved."

"Yes, it is. Thanks to you."

She gave me a quick kiss, then quickly crawled off the bed and rushed into the bathroom. "We're so late."

"I already told you, no one is going to say a word."

"That's not the point," Samantha argued. "Now, hurry up and get ready."

After taking a quick shower, we both got dressed and headed over to the clubhouse. By the time we arrived, everyone was already gathered in the family room. As soon as Blaze spotted us in the doorway, he looked down at his watch and teased, "Hey, Prez. Good to see you finally made it. We were beginning to think you forgot about us."

"Um-hmm. I'm sure you did."

Unable to resist, Riggs poked, "It's okay, Prez. We understand if you had more important places to be."

"You know better than that, Riggs." I glanced around the room at all the brothers as I said, "You all do."

"Yeah, we know," Blaze replied. "But it's not often that we have a reason to give you a hard time."

"Why don't you boys get your president and his woman a drink? It is my birthday after all."

"You got it."

When Blaze went to grab us a couple of beers, I looked over to Samantha. Her eyebrow was cocked high, and I knew exactly what she was thinking. I leaned over and kissed her on the cheek. "Yes. You were right."

"I didn't say a word," she snickered.

"You didn't have to."

Once Blaze gave us our beers, we took a few minutes to say our hellos, then Samantha went over to help the girls get dinner ready. We were just about to sit down to eat, when August and Gunner came over to me. They were expecting their first child in a few months, and August had never looked more beautiful. She was practically beaming as she handed me an envelope and said, "We have something we want to share with you."

"What is it?"

"Open it and see." I tore the envelope open and found a picture of the baby's ultrasound inside. As I looked down at it, August pointed down at the bottom of the picture and said, "We're having a boy."

"Well, how about that. I'm going to have a grandson."

Gunner looked over to me and said, "We've decided to name him Tanner. That way, your family name will carry on with him."

I had so much I wanted to say, but the words wouldn't come. I was too overcome with emotion. I could only stand there and stare at the picture of my soon-to-be grandson. After several moments, August reached over and hugged me. As she held me tight, she whispered, "You mean so much to both of us. Probably more than you realize."

As I hugged her back, I replied, "Thank you. This is the best birthday present I've ever gotten."

I was still hugging August when I felt a tug on my jeans. I released August, and when I looked down, I found Harper staring back up at me. As I knelt down and picked her up, she smiled and said, "Gammy said it's time to eat."

"Well, I guess we better get over there then."

Gunner and August followed us over to the table, and once we sat down, everyone got busy making their plates. As I sat back and looked out at my family, I thought back to the days I started building Memphis chapter. I wasn't just organizing another club. I was assembling a family, one that wasn't defined simply by names or blood. I was choosing men who would value the brotherhood, committing their lives to one another and always remaining loyal, even when it wasn't easy to do so. It wasn't a simple task. There were days when I thought I would surely fail, but as I sat there looking at these men I called *brother*, I knew without a doubt I had succeeded. We were family, through and through, and I took pride in the fact that even after I was dead and gone, the Satan's Fury legacy would still carry on without me. I had done my job, and I had done it well.

THE END

A NOTE FROM L. WILDER

Thanks so much for reading Gus! I had planned on this book being a short novella that followed the excerpt used in the Love, Loyalty, and Mayhem anthology, but Gus demanded more. You will see more of Gus and Samantha in Rider's book that will release later this fall.

If you haven't had a chance to check out Gunner: Satan's Fury MC- Memphis, there is a short excerpt after the acknowledgments.

Also, if you want to know more about Jasper, (Grady's brother) be sure to check out *Day Three: What Bad Boys Do* which is already live on Amazon.

Day Three Blurb:

There's nothing more dangerous than a man with nothing to lose.

The moment I saw Madison Brooks, I knew she was different from the others. She wasn't a hardened criminal with blood on her hands. She was innocent, untouched by my world, and undeniably beautiful.

I couldn't get her out of my head. I kept imagining what it would be like to hold her, touch her, and claim her as mine.

On day three, I found myself questioning whether or not I could complete the assignment. In fact, I found myself questioning everything.

Also coming soon!

For those of you who've been asking about Grady, his book will release later this winter and will include more about Gabriella! You won't want to miss it!

Be sure to sign up for my newsletter for updates on releases and chances to win giveaways. Here's the link: http://eepurl.com/dvSpW5

Also- please follow me on BookBub: https://www.bookbub.com/authors/l-wilder

ACKNOWLEDGMENTS

I am blessed to have so many wonderful people who are willing to give their time and effort to making my books the best they can be. Without them, I wouldn't be able to breathe life into my characters and share their stories with you. To the people I've listed below and so many others, I want to say thank you for taking this journey with me. Your support means the world to me, and I truly mean it when I say appreciate everything you do. I love you all!

PA: Natalie Weston
Editing/Proofing: Lisa Cullinan- editor, Rose Holub- Proofer, Honey Palomino- Proofer
Promoting: Amy Jones, Veronica Ines Garcia, Neringa Neringiukas, Whynter M. Raven, Heather Hungate- Brown, Stracey Charran Ishwar

BETAS/Early Readers: Kaci Stewart, Tanya Skaggs, Jo Lynn, and Jessey Elliott
Street Team: All the wonderful members of Wilder's Women (You rock!)
Best Friend and biggest supporter: My mother (Love you to the moon and back.)

A short excerpt of Gunner: Satan's Fury MC-Memphis Book 5 is included in the following pages. Blaze, Shadow, Riggs, and Murphy are also included in this Memphis series. You can find each of them on Amazon, and they are free with KU.

EXCERPT FROM GUNNER: SATAN'S FURY MC-MEMPHIS

PROLOGUE

When I joined the Marines, I didn't have any preconceived notions about being in the military and going to war. I'd seen and heard enough to know it wasn't going to be easy—far from it. It was one of the hardest, but greatest, things I'd ever done. I worked my ass off, fought for my country, and learned just how far I could be pushed without breaking. But it came at a price. Every waking moment I'd wondered if my time was about to run out, if I'd seen my last sunset or had lain my head down on my pack for the very last time. Even if I'd managed to survive long enough to see the sunrise the next morning, there'd been little consolation in knowing I'd just have to go through that same hell all over again.

I thought I'd find peace once I was finally back in the States with my family and friends and able to sleep in my own bed or walk down the street without feeling like I was under a constant threat—but I'd been wrong. I never realized just how wrong until a shotgun wound forced me to go home.

WHEN I GOT off the plane, I found my mother waiting for me at the gate. As expected, she was alone and still wearing her green Food and More grocery smock. Her tired eyes filled with tears the second she spotted me walking in her direction. "Cade!" she called, rushing towards me with her arms opened wide.

She was just about to reach for me when she suddenly stopped and looked down at my arm. After getting shot in the shoulder, I had to have reconstructive surgery, which meant wearing a sling for the next couple of months. "I'm okay, Mom."

She eased up on her tiptoes and carefully wrapped her arms around my neck, giving me one of her famous mom hugs. Damn. I was a grown man, and her hugs still got to me the same way they did when I was a kid. "I can't tell you how good it is to see you, sweetheart."

"Good to see you too."

"I've been worried sick about you. Your father has too."

"I know." I gave her a quick squeeze, then said, "I'm sorry I worried you."

"I'm just glad you're home where we can take care of you." She gave me a little pat as she stepped back and smiled. "Have to fatten you up a bit."

I was six-four and weighed about two hundred and forty pounds. Before I was shot, I worked out every day and knew what condition I was in. I glanced down at myself and told her, "I'm not exactly skin and bones here, Mom."

"Well, you look like you've lost weight to me ... and you're a little peeked."

"Yeah, well … you'd look a little peeked too if you'd just spent the last sixteen hours on an airplane." Before she could respond, I added, "Let me grab my bag, and then we can get out of here."

As she followed me over to the baggage claim area, she explained, "Your father wanted to come tonight, but you know how he is around crowds. We both figured it would be easier if he just waited at the house for us."

My father was a brilliant man. There wasn't a mathematical problem he couldn't figure out, which made him one of the best accountants in town. But he'd always been a little *different*. He wasn't a fan of crowds or loud noises. He'd fixate on things from historical facts to the changes in weather, obsessing on every detail, and he wasn't exactly big on showing affection—except for when he was with my mother. He'd always been different with her— touching her, holding her hand, and even hugging her. I'd always hoped that some of that would rub off on me, but it never did. "It's fine, Mom. I wasn't expecting him to be here."

"Well, he's really looking forward to seeing you."

Even though I knew that wasn't true, I replied, "I'm looking forward to seeing him too."

"Oh, and Brooklyn should be home by the time we get there."

As I lifted my duffle-bag off the conveyer belt, I asked, "She been making it okay?"

"You know your sister … she's always on the go." Mom shrugged. "But I guess that's a good thing. It keeps her out of trouble."

We headed outside to the parking garage, and once we got to Mom's car, she popped the trunk and I tossed my bag inside. I slammed it shut and then we both got in the car and started home. We hadn't been driving long when I heard her let out a deep sigh. I glanced over at her, and even in the dark, I could see the dark circles under her eyes. "Have you been working double shifts again?"

"No ... it's just been a long week."

"Why's that?"

"Let's not talk about that right now," she interrupted, then quickly changed the subject. "I've got your room all ready for you and got your rehab appointments all lined up. CJ and Dalton are planning to come by and see you once you get settled."

"That'd be cool."

It had been years since I'd seen my best friends from high school. We'd all gone our separate ways, so I was surprised when she said, "Did you know that CJ and his girlfriend, Adeline, are expecting?"

"Hadn't heard that."

"I don't think it was something they were planning, but ... you know how those things go."

Mom continued to ramble on about all the latest gossip in town until we pulled up in the driveway. As soon as she'd parked, I got out, grabbed my bag, and followed her up to the front door. She motioned for me to go inside as she said, "You get settled, and I'll go start dinner. I'm making pork chops and mashed potatoes."

"Okay, sounds good." When I walked into the living room, I found Dad sitting in his recliner with his TV tray in front of him. He was studying one of his patches through a magnifying glass, something I'd seen him do a thousand times before. It was a hobby that started when he was a kid. In hopes of helping him make friends, his folks had signed him up for the Boy Scouts. While their plan for him to make friends didn't pan out, he did gain an interest in patches. That interest turned into an obsession—an obsession that carried over into his adulthood. He didn't even look up when I walked over to him. "Hey, Pop. How's it going?"

"Good."

I swallowed back the feeling of rejection that was creeping up inside of me and tried once again to get his attention. "You get some new patches?"

"Um-hmm." Without turning to look at me, he held up the long, narrow patch and said, "It's an Unteroffizier-vorschule cuff title."

"I got no idea what that is, Pop."

Like he was reading straight from the encyclopedia, he spouted off, "*Unteroffiziervorschule* is German for NCO Preparatory School. The German military created the school to train lower ranks in leadership and initiative. Their students eventually became commissioned officers."

"Wow, that's really something."

"Also found a set of World War II German rural police collar tabs.

"Oh, really?" There was a time when it bothered me that my father showed me little to no attention, but as I grew older, I realized that it wasn't his fault. My father had Asperger's Syndrome. I had no choice but to accept the fact that he'd never be the kind of father I hoped he would be. "Are those good ones?"

Like a child, he brought it close to his body, protecting it as he answered, "Yes. Very good."

"That's great, Pop." As I started towards my room, I told him, "I'm gonna go get settled in." Without replying, he turned his attention back to his magnifying glass, and just like always, it was like I'd never been in the room.

I went upstairs to my room and lay across the bed. As I stared up at my old Bon Jovi poster, I was surprised by how different it felt to be here. Everything was exactly the way I'd left it, but for some reason, everything in the whole fucking house seemed different. What had once felt like home was now completely foreign to me.

Over the next few days that feeling had only grown stronger. When my buddies from high school had come by to see me, it was like they were complete strangers. After the first few minutes, the conversations became forced and awkward. I couldn't even talk to my mother and sister. It was like I was stuck inside my head and couldn't find the right words to say to anyone. I'd told myself it would pass, that things would get back to normal eventually, but they didn't. With each new day, things only seemed to get be getting worse. Hell, even the shit with my father was fucking with my head. He'd never talked to me or showed that he gave a damn about me, and I'd adapted to that. I'd stopped hoping that things would change, but I could feel the resentment building inside of me, making me feel like I was going to explode at any minute. I just couldn't take it. I needed to get the fuck out of that house and out of my head, or I was going to lose my mind. I grabbed my keys and headed downstairs. Just as I was about to walk out the front door, Mom called out to me, "Cade? Wait! Where are you going?"

"I'm going out."

"Again?" Confusion crossed her face. "Is something wrong?"

"No, Mom. I'm just—"

She gave me one of her looks as she interrupted, "You're just *what*, Cade?"

"I can't do this anymore. It's just too much."

"What are you talking about? What's too much?"

"*Everything*. This house. This town." I let out an aggravated breath as I grumbled, "*Dad*."

"I know it's not easy coming home after all you've been through, but we love you, sweetheart. We like having you here with us."

"Why do you keep saying *we*?" I huffed. "Dad could care less if I'm alive or dead."

"That's not true, Cade. Your father loves you."

I shook my head as I argued, "Yeah, right. He's never once given me a second thought, and you damn well know it."

"Come with me. I want to show you something." She walked into my dad's office and over to the glass case where he kept his prized patches. As she opened the top latch, she explained, "A few days after you left for training, your father started a new collection."

I glanced down at the case and my chest tightened as soon as I saw it was lined with various Marine Corp patches, from the seal and crest to old veteran patches. "There's so many of them."

"I know, honey. He might not be good at showing it, but you've been on his mind every day."

I could feel the emotion building inside of me as I muttered, "I didn't know."

"I know." Mom had always understood my father in a way I never could. As far as I could tell, my father had never given me a second thought, but as she stood there staring down at those patches, she seemed to think otherwise. She slipped her arm around my back, doing her best to reassure me as she said, "That's why I wanted you to see this."

It meant a lot to me to see those patches, to know that I'd crossed my father's mind. That realization made me feel like the walls were closing in on me. I couldn't breathe. I needed to get some air before I totally lost it. I leaned over and kissed her cheek. "I'll be back in a couple of hours."

I rushed out of the house, got in my truck, and cranked the engine. There was only one place for me to escape the thoughts that were rushing through my head —Danver's Pub. When I walked in, it looked exactly how it did five years ago. They were even playing the same damn songs on the jukebox, but I didn't give a rat's ass about the music or the décor. I needed a fucking drink. Hell, I needed a slew of them. I went over to the counter, placed my order for three shots of chilled vodka, and downed them one right after the other. I ordered three more, immediately knocking them down, and was about to order three more when a man came over and sat down next to me. I took a quick glance at him and an uneasy feeling washed over me when I saw that he was wearing a Satan's Fury cut. Their MC was known for being a group of badasses who didn't take shit from anyone, and from the looks of the patch he was sporting, this guy next to me was the biggest badass of them all. He was a big guy, maybe in his late forties, but he was fit and looked like he could hold his own and then some. He called the bartender over and said, "Bring us another round."

The bartender nodded, then placed six shot glasses on

the counter, quickly filling them to the brim. "Anything else?"

"For now, … just keep my tab running." He lifted one of the shot glasses and asked, "You got a name, kid?"

"Cade."

"Couldn't help but notice the military cut. You in the service?"

"I was." I ran my hand over the top of my head as I replied, "I just got back a few days ago."

"Well, here's to you, Cade. Thanks for your service." He motioned his hand towards my round of shots and waited for me to lift mine, and then we both threw them back. "So, you got plans to go back?"

"Nah. Pretty sure that chapter of my life has closed. My shoulder guaranteed that."

"What's up with your shoulder?"

"Bullet fucked up my rotator cuff."

"Damn." He shook his head as he reached for another shot. "That's a tough one, but you're young, you'll be back like new before you know it."

"You sound pretty sure of yourself."

"That's because I am," he said, then he pulled back the sleeve of his t-shirt, revealing a wound similar to mine. "Hurt like a bitch, but eventually healed and so will yours."

"Good to know." I took another shot, then immediately reached for the next. "Thanks for the round."

"Least I can do. After all, you seem pretty damn determined to get tanked tonight, so I thought I'd help you out."

"Needed to clear my head."

"Vodka isn't gonna help you with that."

"Maybe not, but after the day I've had, it's worth a try."

"Been one of those days, huh?"

"Yeah," I muttered. "You could say that."

"Life has a way of throwing some pretty hard punches … some harder than others." He looked me dead in the eye. "You've just gotta take the hit and find a way to get back up."

"I've had one too many hits, man. Not sure I see the point in getting back up anymore."

"Put your hand on your heart." He waited silently as I did as he requested. "You feel that? As long as your heart's beating, then you've got a purpose. You've just gotta figure out what it is."

"I'm trying, but it's just so damn hard." I ran my hand down my face and sighed. "Every fucking thing is exactly the same as it was when I left … my folks, my house, this whole damn city, but it feels so different. How is that possible?"

"Because you've changed. You can't expect things to be the same when you're not the same man you were when you left."

"I'm still me, though."

"Yeah, but now you're a different version of yourself." His eyes narrowed as he asked, "You ever ridden before?"

"A motorcycle?"

"Not talking about a fucking moped, son," he scoffed.

I shrugged. "Ridden a couple of times when I was younger but never actually had one of my own."

"Might be time to try again."

"Maybe so."

"*Maybe* isn't an answer, son." Then he leaned towards me and said, "If I've learned anything in this life, it's that we only regret the chances we didn't take. It's time for you to take that chance."

"I hear ya." I reached for my last shot and added, "But I don't own a motorcycle, and even if I did, I couldn't ride with this shoulder."

"That's two problems, son." He chuckled. "Both can be solved with time."

He reached into his pocket, pulled out a card, and offered it to me. "The name's Gus. When you get back on your feet, come by the clubhouse. We'll take that ride together."

"Sounds good. I'll do that."

"I'll be looking forward to it." After finishing off his last shot, he stood up and started to walk away. "Drink to your heart's content. Just be sure to get a ride home, son."

"Will do."

There was something about the way he'd called me *son* that got to me. As odd as it seemed, it felt like he actually meant it. Until that moment, I hadn't realized how much I needed to hear it. That one word had me looking down at the card Gus had given me, and I knew at that moment I would be taking that ride with him. What I didn't know was how that decision would change my life forever.

GUNNER

"Give me a second," I called out to Blaze. "I'll be right back."

"Whoa … Where are you going?" His eyes narrowed as he watched me start across the parking lot. "We're going to be late."

I was following Blaze, Shadow, Murphy, and their ol' ladies into the gas station when a gorgeous brunette in the parking lot caught my attention. She was pacing back and forth in front of her car. I couldn't tell for sure, but it looked like she was crying as she talked to someone on her cell phone. When we came back out and she was still there, I figured something must be wrong. There was something about a woman in need that got to me, especially when she was smoking hot with curves made for sin. As I continued walking towards her, I glanced back at Blaze and said, "No, we won't. I'll just be a minute."

"Um-hmm. I've heard that shit before," he complained. Murphy, the club's sergeant-at-arms, was a good guy, always played by the rules and never let a brother down, so I wasn't surprised when he said, "We still gotta drop the girls off, and if we're late for church, Gus is gonna be pissed."

"I already told ya ... We won't be late."

As I made my way closer to the woman, I heard her say, "Are you sure about this?" A gust of wind whipped passed us, and I quickly became mesmerized by the way her long, dark hair fluttered around her face. Damn. It was like I'd been pulled into some romantic, chick flick where everything was moving in slow motion. I needed to shake it off before I made a fucking fool of myself. She tucked her hair behind her ears as she continued, "I'm not certain. I think I'm close, but I took the wrong exit. Don't worry, I'll figure it out." After another brief pause, she said, "I'll let you know."

When she ended the call, I put on my best smile and asked, "You lost, darlin'?"

The gorgeous brunette glanced up at me for a moment, and her dark eyes quickly drifted over me. Clearly unaffected by my dashing good looks, she looked down at her phone and replied, "No."

"You sure about that ... 'cause you're a long way from heaven."

I cocked my head to the side and smiled, hoping she'd find the humor in my corny pickup line. Sadly, she was totally unfazed. Instead, my words just hung in the air, completely disregarded as she stared down at her phone. "I'm sure you're a nice enough guy and all, but I really don't have time for this right now."

"Okay, then. Tell me how I can help." I wasn't sure what to make of her. I knew she wasn't from around here, otherwise she'd know how dangerous it was for her to be standing out in the parking lot with every thug around checking her out. I couldn't blame them. Hell, she looked like a knockout in those hip-hugging jeans and low-cut t-shirt. I could only imagine what she'd look like wearing nothing at all. Just the thought made it difficult not to readjust myself. Unfortunately, I didn't have the same effect on her. In fact, she seemed unimpressed by my southern charm and was doing her best to disregard me completely. I could've just walked away, kept what was left of my ego intact, but that would have been too easy. "Seriously … you got any idea where you are?"

"Actually, I do. I'm in Memphis and"—she glanced up at the store front sign— "at the Citgo gas station on Frayser Road."

"So, you know you're in Frayser?"

"Umm … Yeah." Her eyebrows furrowed as she asked, "Why?"

"Not exactly safe around here, darlin'." I lifted my chin, motioning my head towards the hood-rats smoking dope at the side of the building. "There are some real bad folks around these parts."

Her gazed drifted downward as she took a moment to study my torn jeans, leather cut, and tattoos. She shook her head, then clipped, "And what about you? Are you one of them?"

"Depends on who you ask."

"Um-hmm. If had to guess, I would say you and your friends are just as dangerous, *if not more so*, as those men over there." With a cocked brow and a half-smile, she sassed, "Regardless, I'd already be gone if you weren't here … *you know*, distracting me."

"Well, that's as much your fault as it is mine." I let my

eyes slowly drift over her, taking my time to study every gorgeous inch of her, as I said, "If you weren't so damn beautiful, I wouldn't be over here talking to you. Besides, I had to at least try and see if there was something I could do to help. Wouldn't want anything to happen to you while you were out here all alone."

"You're good. I'll give you that." She shook her head and scoffed, "A regular knight in shining armor, but you're wasting your time with me. I'm fine."

"I don't know about that." A smirk crossed my face as I added, "This is no place for someone like you, so if you're lost, I'll be glad to help you find wherever it is you're trying to go."

"Thanks, but I think I've got it figured out." She got in her car, and just before she closed her door, she looked over to me and said, "Maybe you'll have better luck with your next damsel in distress."